You can contact Simon Herfet at his website at:

https://simonherfetauthor.wordpress.com/

OTHER BOOKS BY SIMON HERFET;

'Awakening to love' – A channelled book about the Spiritual Relationship to Consciousness, Universal Love and Awareness. Published by Balboa Press.

'Awakening to Love' Book 2: A channelled book about How to trust in Love and Relinquish Fear to Help Humanity Live in Global Unity. Available on Amazon.

Six Dancing Dolphins

A Story to Help You Remember
What You always Knew

SIMON HERFET

Papa Luca, walked into the Galley Café in the old picturesque sea-side town and ordered his usual drink at the counter, "I'll have a ginger beer with ice please," he said to the waitress.

"Sure," the young waitress replied, she took and poured out the drink from the bottle and handed him the iced drink still fizzing.

"Thank you", said Papa Luca, to the young waitress, looking her straight in the eyes with a warm and friendly smile.

He went to sit down at a table in the corner of the café, where surf boards adorned the walls and some were suspended and hanging from the ceiling, however, none were for sale as the café proprietor was in love with his surf-boards as they had brought him so much joy on the ocean waves.

Papa Luca, turned and started to speak with a young man named Joshua, he was about thirty years of age and was sat opposite him at the same table.

Joshua, said to Papa Luca, who had been a close friend of his father before he had died several years earlier, "Why did you call me and ask me to meet you here Papa Luca?"

Papa Luca replied, "Because you called to me in your dreams to come and speak to you, to help you face and deal with some of the difficulties which await you now in this life and to help you understand them. There will be many challenges and many adventures to come sometimes with joy, sometimes sadness."

The young man looked confused at Papa Luca and a wave of anxiety seemed to engulf his being. Joshua, had lived a normal life until this meeting with the strange and mysterious man, even though he had been his father's friend and besides he barely even knew him, he thought to himself.

Through the misted single window-pane, Joshua, could see the passers-by with their hoods up, or carrying umbrellas to protect themselves from the autumn rain outside.

The young man asked Papa Luca, "So, why have you asked me here, to speak to you now, after all this time. I barely even know you do I?"

Papa Luca, looked different to Joshua, not as he remembered him, they had last met when Joshua was still only a boy. Papa Luca was about sixty years of age, with long grey hair tied back into a ponytail, he had a short grey beard and was casually dressed in a modern conventional style. But it was the bright blue sparkling eyes of Papa Luca which stared deeply into the Joshua's soul in a loving fatherly way which confused Joshua the most, it was as if Joshua somehow was connected to Papa Luca, but at the same time he realised that he knew very little about him or his life. Why would he as he was only a boy when they had met last, he thought to himself.

Papa Luca, said to him slowly in a deep loving tone,

"Joshua, before your father died I made him a promise that I would help you if the need were to arise, even if just to help guide you in times of transition. Now is such a time for many, as many changes will soon be engulfing this world and as you will soon see. But first you have some journeys to make to various places to help prepare you for the changes which will soon come, you have much to do and face in your life ahead. Do not be afraid, for all will turn out well. You will battle your own inner demons and in the future, you will get married and then have several children. They will bring you much joy and heart-break but life is never a smooth path Joshua".

Papa Luca, touched Joshua's arm as he spoke. Joshua thought of the future. He was shown in his mind what he knew was the future, his future just as Papa

Luca was telling him – visions simultaneously appeared in his mind, as if by magic.

After about an hour of speaking but what felt like five minutes, Papa Luca said to Joshua, "It is time to go but I will return. We will speak more in the future as I have been sent here to help you awaken your consciousness to who you really are and to help you cross the ravine of your fear and anxiety to the love and confidence which lies on the other side. Until we meet again Joshua – which will be soon, I bid you, adieu!"

With that Papa Luca got up and left the café in silence.

***

Joshua, went to a cupboard, which was in an old bedroom where he spent so much of his time when at home. He reached and took from the drawer a map which had gathered dust as it had been sat at the bottom of the drawer for a very long time. He had looked at it before after finding it many years earlier under some lining paper in the drawer of the old cupboard but due to a lack of interest then merely returned it to where he found it for another time should he wish to investigate its meaning in the future. He could not make any sense of the map or its purpose even though he sensed that it somehow contained a message for him. It appeared to show a section of coastline near to where he lived with diagrams written on it with a red cross scrawled on it by someone at the entry point to an estuary on the shoreline shown on it and near to where Joshua lived. Joshua looked more closely at the map now spread out in front of him. There was little writing on the map – what there was, was written in black ink in calligraphy and he knew it had to be quite old. Joshua wondered what the cross marked in red might mean. Could the 'x' mark the spot of some treasure on a sunken ship he wondered to himself, almost in the hope of creating his own kind of adventure?

He folded the map up carefully and placed it back in the cupboard drawer where he had found it originally and went about his usual business for the day, still thinking about the mysterious cross written upon the map he had found.

Joshua thought to himself, 'Everyone is looking for their own buried treasure, not knowing what it is, or where exactly they might find it and so he thought perhaps the map to him was simply only a metaphor for the treasure many people search for often in their own hearts.

***

Joshua, found he had to spend time everyday outside to get some exercise and to commune with nature and to breath in the fresh sea air in the town where he lived by the coast and a place that had been home to many adventurers down the ages. Many past inhabitants of the old town had been sailors who had set off in their youth with many never returning. Some had returned with their many tales of adventure and intrigue, tales of distant shores visited and of the different, sometimes strange people, that they had met on their many travels.

Joshua, often thought and dreamed of being a maritime adventurer, sailing the high-seas and of pirate escapades and such, or of being the captain of his own square-rigger sailing ship, setting off on adventures far, far away. However, as much as the sea drew him, it also scared him, for he knew it had been the cause of much human loss and misery through the course of time and so he deeply respected its power as well as its beauty.

***

The next day as Joshua walked into his house he noticed that it felt different for some reason, he said to his mother who was eighty-three years old, "What has happened in this house? It feels different for some reason."

"I have cleaned it! I know it doesn't happen often!" She replied, laughing at the same time.

"No, how right you are!" Joshua said laughing back at her as he spoke and wondering at the same time if he would ever be able to find his most treasured belongings ever again including his old map, of the coastline nearby.

He said to his mother, "What have you done with my things mum?"

"What things"? she replied.

"My walking boots and clothing," Joshua replied.

"Oh, those, they are under the stairs now," she replied.

"Okay, thanks," said Joshua, relieved that he knew where they were, so he could make a quick getaway in the morning as he had a plan and something special was starting the next day for Joshua. His life would never be the same again. He had a dream the night before about six dancing dolphins – and he had an idea!

***

The next morning, Joshua woke up early. He drew back his bedroom curtains and looked outside. The sun was shining gloriously so he threw on his old clothes and after a quick breakfast of porridge and tea strolled down to the scenic harbour near where he lived and where he had spent most of the thirty years of his life so far.

At the quay-side he met Harry, an old family friend. Harry, always had a twinkle in his eye and knew the sea well, having grown up there and was one of the best fisherman in the area and almost being able to sustain if he chose to, half of the small town with his daily catches of fish.

"How are you today Harry?" asked Joshua.

"Great, where are we off to today then Joshua?" Harry replied.

Then continued, "You said this was going to be a special trip, an adventure."

"Yes, I do hope so. I found an old map in a drawer at home. I think it could lead us to something special. Head west to the fourth estuary along the coast, just before the point, okay." Joshua said hastily.

"All right, Joshua, I hope you know what you are doing? I have got the entire day free today, which is good," said Harry.

Harry started up the old diesel engine of the small fishing boat and headed west. The sun was shining and off they set out of the quiet and small harbour, right around the harbour wall and hugging close into the shoreline as they went.

"So, what are we searching for?" Harry enquired.

Joshua paused for a while deep in thought. Then he slowly said, "Harry, you know in life we are all searching for our own treasure, of one sort or another, metaphorically speaking, don't you think?"

"Yes, I guess so," Harry replied with a frown.

Joshua continued, "The thing is most of us just don't know what it is, do we? For some it is lots of money. For others, it is that special love of another person. Then for some people it is just living a healthy peaceful life. For me, it has always been searching for an adventure to help me find the secrets to life I guess!"

"You can say that again. You always seem to be searching for something or other. Why don't you just wait for once. Maybe then, what you are seeking will be able to find you?" Harry said, tentatively.

Joshua stopped what he was doing and looked at Harry, smiled and said, "How come you always speak with such wisdom Harry? I think you are probably right. I know I need to slow down a bit even though I am only thirty years of age. It is just that I feel there is some important secret about life, I have yet to discover!"

Harry replied, "Why on earth do you think this time, it lies at the bottom of the sea, where an 'x' is marked on an old map? Do you think it is sunken treasure, or something in the ocean? There won't be any wrecks by that estuary you spoke of. All the big undiscovered wrecks are way out at sea!" said Harry.

"Yes, I know. But I found this old local shoreline map in my cupboard. I had never noticed it until recently, as it was under the lining paper at the bottom of a drawer. I thought it would be an adventure to go out to the estuary as I have never been there before, just to look. How long will it take to get there, Harry?" Joshua replied.

"About a couple of hours," said Harry, somewhat phased by Joshua's unrealistic expectation of finding something where boats pass every day, notwithstanding the fact that neither of them were scuba-diving experts. In any case, they had no such equipment at their disposal.

They sat together quietly enjoying the vista both sides of the boat as they journeyed onwards. On one side, there was an abundant green shoreline and on the other side of the boat a view only of the deep blue horizon where the sea disappeared into nothingness.

A couple of seagulls a few feet above them made a squawking noise hoping for a piece of fish to be thrown their way. Harry threw them a slither of mackerel flesh which one of the gulls caught in mid-air and both the men on the boat laughed simultaneously at the acrobatic antics of the ever-hungry gulls.

"So, Joshua what is this treasure that you are seeking?" Asked Harry, looking Joshua square in the eyes as he did so.

"I'm not sure really Harry. All my life I feel that I have been looking to discover who I really am. I suppose I look in the mirror each day and I see someone looking back but I don't feel that is who I really am. The flesh and blood before me, is part of who I am, but not all of me. I am looking for the rest of me I suppose. The part that alludes me still. That is what I am searching for I guess," replied Joshua.

"Oh, right, and you think you might find it here in the sea, just at the mouth of any ordinary estuary. Just because you found a map with an 'x' on it, marking the spot of something or other, do you?" said Harry.

Joshua replied, "Yes, I suppose I do strangely. I think maybe I will find something there that will reveal more about the mystery of who I really am. Who we all are really."

"Okay, but what I don't understand is how on earth you think you could possibly find that in the ocean somehow?" asked Harry quizzically.

"I know. Nor do I," replied Joshua. With that both men sat back in silence. Harry watched the other boats course in front of the boat and Joshua looked at the lush undergrowth which reached down to the sea-shore as the little fishing boat continued to chug westwards along the shore-line and half a mile or so, out from the beach.

***

Eventually they arrived at the estuary. The fourth estuary along to the west from the small harbour and focal point of their small home town.

Harry said to Joshua, "Right, this is it and we are slap bang in the estuary mouth's entrance here Joshua. The tide will be on the turn soon and it will be harder to hold the boat in this position. What are you going to do about the prospect of us both being right above your maps cross, now then?"

"Nothing, I never was planning to do anything Harry," replied Joshua.

"What do you mean, you were never planning to do anything once here? So, we have taken two hours or so to sail out here for nothing then, have we Joshua?" said Harry, with an angry tone in his voice.

"No, not for nothing Harry. We have had a nice relaxing couple of hours sailing to get here, haven't we!" said Joshua a bit sheepishly.

"Right, but I had a lot of other things, that I needed to get on with today really!" Harry replied sternly.

"You should have said so!" Joshua retorted.

"Oh, well there is always another day, I suppose," said Harry reticently.

"Exactly," replied Joshua.

"Anyway, you reckon we are right over this elusive 'x' mark now, do you Harry?" asked Joshua.

"Yes, I do reckon," said Harry, in his characteristic west country drawl.

As both men stared at each other, Joshua noticed a big grin break out across Harry's bearded face and with the wind blowing through his long grey curly hair as he smiled, Harry excitedly said, "Quick turn around and look down by your side of the boat. What can you see?"

"A dolphin, I just saw it – a large dolphin just surfaced. I saw its dorsal fin break the surface and dive back down again. How amazing is that?" Joshua said with great excitement in his voice.

Harry was used to seeing dolphins in the summer as he was always out at sea fishing in his boat. Joshua however, much as he loved the sea, seldom managed to get out on a boat due to his sea-sickness problem, which often happened to him when he did get out to sea. So, he had hardly ever seen a wild dolphin swimming as he did at that moment, he felt so ecstatic at seeing it free in the ocean.

As they both kept their gaze fixed on the spot where the dolphin had disappeared into the sea's depths then suddenly in the next moment, the dolphin reappeared again, this time the beautiful creature popped up his head fully above the water's surface and made a squeaking noise at them both and showing its teeth, as if it was smiling at them both simultaneously. As it did so, the dolphin flipped its two flippers frantically to keep its head above the water long enough to make the brief encounter memorable to them all. No sooner had it appeared, it disappeared back down into the ocean's depths.

Harry laughed. Joshua looked down at the water's surface in awe and disbelief. Then swiftly turned to Harry and said, "How amazing was that Harry. It was as if it came to say 'hello' to us. As if to say, "Thanks for coming guys – nice to see you both. Wasn't it Harry?"

"Yeah, just what I was thinking – the 'x' definitely marked the spot!" replied Harry.

Both men sat down on the boats side-bench, built into the boats hull, still in awe of what they had just seen. They both thought about the synchronicity of the moment to themselves.

Joshua, thought of the deeper meaning and simply how lucky they both had been to be there on the boat in that moment. He forgot at that time that an 'x' marked the spot on the dusty old map still lying at the bottom of the drawer back home.

***

The next day Joshua woke up early. He went downstairs and sat at the old wooden kitchen table and started to drink his freshly made tea. He was still thinking about the previous day and the dolphin experience. He wondered about the synchronicity of the moment. The fact the enigmatic creature had popped up its head from the water's surface, as if to say 'hello', right at the spot they had journeyed out to. He wondered if perhaps it was no coincidence at all and that maybe the reason for the dolphin appearing in that moment was to show both Harry and him that nothing happens by coincidence, and that perhaps everything happens for a reason. Joshua, continued to enjoy his cup of tea and tried to give his mind a rest for a short time, something he often found difficult to do. After about ten minutes of sitting in the kitchen and trying to rest his mind from thinking he decided that he was feeling bored of sitting and just trying not to think so he went back up to his bedroom and opened the old cupboard draw and lifted the old map out and placed it on the bed to examine it more closely. There was no date on it and although it looked very old to Joshua and because he was not a cartographer, he could not tell exactly how old the map was, it was a fact which eluded him. He placed the old map carefully back into the drawer and decided to go for a walk to see a friend, someone older and wiser than himself and who had also been a friend of his own father, before he had passed away.

Joshua's own father, was a difficult man to get along with and was not very good in social situations. He had a difficult time in the Second World War and because he had been taken prisoner towards the end in 1944 and had been held captive. Although, by all accounts he was treated well by his German captors, it was not something he chose to speak about often. It was a time, he simply chose to forget, like many of the other war veterans.

Joshua walked down through the main street of the old towns central shopping area. Ahead was the view out across the sea to the distant contoured cliffs, clearly visible. The sun was sparkling like a thousand tiny diamonds on the sea's surface, Joshua turned left into the lounge bar of The Lion Hotel, one of the oldest buildings in the town. There in the corner of the bar as he had hoped, sat at a table, was another of his father's old friends called Tom, who was sat drinking a cup of tea and reading a book. He didn't notice Joshua, as he quietly walked over towards him and placed his right hand on Tom's right shoulder, as Tom was sat with his back to the lounge bar door, he did not see Joshua walk in but said to him, however, "Hello Joshua, I sensed you coming to visit me a short while ago. How can I help you this time?"

Joshua sat down at the small wooden table where Tom was sat. The old sash window next to them was slightly open allowing a small amount of fresh air and street noise to filter into the room. Tom looked over the top of his reading glasses and looked at Joshua, with a fondness as if he was his own son, Tom had no children of his own, sadly for him.

"So, what can I do for you, Joshua?" Tom asked.

"How did you know I was coming then Tom?" Joshua enquired.

"I knew because I sensed your energy drawing near. I try to be in the moment as much as possible, as you know. Even though at the time, I was reading my book. I could sense your energy and you popped into my mind. We are all connected don't forget – as I have told you many times before Joshua. How can I help you?" replied Tom.

Joshua looked quizzically at Tom's face. Tom had curly grey hair to his shoulders and wore an old beige corduroy shirt that was fraying at the edges of the collar from years of wear, together with an old pair of faded denim dungarees with a pair of walking boots which had paint stains on both from his passion for painting oil landscapes.

Joshua proceeded to tell 'old' Tom all about the previous day's events – the boat down to the estuary and the old map and the magical dolphin's appearance. Joshua wondered if 'old' Tom would see a significance to the events that Joshua had not seen, perhaps? Joshua, was sure that there was more to it than meets the eye! A deeper lesson for him to learn from the experience.

***

'Old' Tom looked over the top of his spectacles intently at Joshua, and asked him, "You want to know the significance of these events, the map, which led to the boat trip to the estuary with Harry and the appearance of the dolphin, where 'x' marked the spot on the same map? Do you not Joshua?"

"Yes, was the appearance of the dolphin just a coincidence? Do you think Tom?" replied Joshua.

Tom paused for a moment, then replied, "What is a coincidence, Joshua?"

Joshua replied, "I would say it is when things occur randomly, yet with a seeming significance. Even though there might be no significance to the events."

Tom replied, "Good answer Joshua. However, I would say differently; that nothing happens by coincidence. This is because at the deepest level, all of creation is connected. There is a knowingness behind all events, even though such might not be known to our conscious minds."

"What is this knowingness then Tom? Where does it come from? What is this mysterious knowingness that you are talking of? Where is it? I don't see much evidence of such Tom," said Joshua, starting to ramble on a bit too much for Tom's liking.

Tom spoke to Joshua softly and deliberately lowering his voice, due to other customers sat at the table close to them in the lounge bar of the hotel, and said,

"Joshua, just because you cannot see something, does not mean, it does not exist! There is a life force. An energy, an intelligence, a love, which is the wisdom and power behind all that you see. That dolphin was aware of your presence while you were both on the boat on the surface of the ocean above it. The dolphin felt a sense to surface at that exact spot – at that exact time – when you were there with Harry. It appeared and in its own way came to you both to say 'hello' through its mere presence and appearance there then and to show you both that the universe was listening to your own small adventure.

The first lesson here, is that the universe is always listening. It reveals this back to you. Especially, when you are listening too!

It is an acknowledgement that we are all plugged in to the universal matrix of consciousness!"

Joshua paused, and looked at Tom and said, "That is pretty deep. But, I think I understand the meaning now. I find the prospect of that pretty exciting Tom, because it means there is a lot more to life than meets the eye, than most suppose there is, doesn't it?"

To which Tom simply replied, "Yes, right Joshua. We are more than meets the eye, for the eyes are truly as they say – the windows to the soul. So, look others in the eyes as much as you can – then, and only then, will you truly be able to see who they really are!"

Joshua thanked Tom for the wisdom he had offered to him and his teaching and bid him farewell and left him in peace to drink his tea. As Joshua walked back up the street he reflected on Tom's teaching that he had just received from him.

Joshua thought to himself that if we are all connected – then we must all have some mysterious force connecting us and sustaining us all. Perhaps, right down to the deepest level of our being. Both physically and spiritually. That perhaps we do all have a soul and maybe our souls experience lots of lives and this is just one. Then, if that is the case, inside of us all there is a part of us that is eternal.

Joshua, came back to the present moment and carefully looked both ways before he crossed the town's busy main street.

***

Papa Luca was waiting for Joshua as he walked inside the café. He too, had heard about Joshua's meeting with the dolphin when out on the boat with Harry.

"A pot of tea with soya milk please," said Joshua to the waitress behind the counter. "That will be two pounds and twenty-five pence please," said the waitress. Joshua paid for his tea and walked carrying it on a tray to a table with an elderly man already sitting there reading a book. Joshua did not immediately recognise Papa Luca from their previous meeting and sat down oblivious with his pot of tea until the old man looked up over his glasses and said to him, "Hello Joshua, I have heard about your meeting with the dolphin the other day."

Joshua looked up as he was pouring his tea into the china cup. "Ah, Papa Luca, how nice to see you again. It feels a bit like you are following me or somehow know my movements before I do. You keep popping up in these unexpected places."

Papa Luca replied, "I know but you see I know you far better than you realise, Joshua."

"Anyway, what did you think about your meeting with the dolphin? It was an auspicious meeting you know! To come that close to and seeing such a beautiful and clever creature," said Papa Luca.

"Really, I know that dolphins are supposed to be very clever creatures but I did not know it was supposed to be auspicious to meet one out in the wild like Harry and I did the other day. Why is it auspicious then?" Joshua replied.

Papa Luca looked at Joshua with his eyes radiating a knowingness and wisdom gained from his long life and his own experiences and said to Joshua,

"Because, nothing happens by coincidence, Joshua. The universe is not a place of random events of chaos. Rather a place of synchronistic events – it is just that most people do not recognise them when they occur.

You went out that day on your boat to 'x' marks the spot on your map wondering what it might lead to. What you found was a beautiful display of nature in the exquisite form of a dolphin jumping out of the water and therefore performing for both of you in a display of nature's wisdom."

Joshua looked at Papa Luca quizzically, still thinking that he did not know him really. Yet, he felt as if he had always known him.

Papa Luca continued, "Joshua, when a dolphin comes to you in the wild it is auspicious because of the spiritual aspect or meaning between the two of you. The dolphin in its playfulness is saying 'hello' to that similar part of you within yourself. The young fun loving and playful part of your character which we are in touch with when we are young but tend to lose our connection to as we get older".

Joshua looked at Papa Luca deep in the eyes for a moment, as if looking into his own eyes. Then he replied to the old man, with the long wavy grey hair, "Yes, I know what you mean. I am thirty years old now and I feel already as if I have left the 'child' part of me behind now. I lost him some time ago. I forget when it was and now I find it difficult to reconnect with that part of me which once found it easy and natural to be playful!"

Papa Luca replied, "Yes, you see Joshua, that is what the dolphin, in part came to teach you! To remind you to go and be a child again – to have fun and play and to release your fears and your worries. You spend so much time in their company, Joshua. Most people do, I know. But, a big part of the reason for that is because people find it hard to keep their own connection with their own inner-child!"

Joshua replied, "Yes, you're right. Harry, is good at that he always has a twinkle in his eye for some reason. He doesn't seem to worry about too much to me. I have noticed in life that those who inspire me most, are often not the wisest of souls, as many appear miserable too. But, those who take life lightly, laugh a lot and hardly ever seem to worry. Almost as if they don't know the meaning of that word."

Papa Luca replied, "Yes, you are quite right. We are all here for only a short time in life. Life goes quickly. You will learn this truth more fully, as you yourself grow older. Each year often seems to pass quicker than the previous one."

Joshua, looked again into Papa Luca's eyes, holding his stare. It had taken Joshua all his life to be able to keep eye contact, it had been as if some mysterious force had prevented him from doing so in his past somehow. He could see more deeply into another's soul now much more clearly than he could previously.

Papa Luca seemed to show an element of telepathy too, towards Joshua, as he seemed to know always what was on Joshua's mind.

At that moment, Papa Luca said, "Eye contact is important Joshua – because then you are connecting at a deeper level to whoever you are speaking to at the time."

Joshua replied, "Yes, I am finding that to be so. But, back to the dolphins. Are they also aware of things on a deeper level? Are they more intuitive than humans do you think?"

Papa Luca paused for a moment, before replying to Joshua's question. "No, dolphins are not more intuitive.

But, because they are without worry. It is not in their nature. They are more playful naturally and therefore more aware of the moment and display more childlike qualities in their playfulness. They are more in touch with the present moment and their surroundings. That is why it jumped out at the exact spot in the moment in time that you found yourself to be where 'x' marked the spot on your map. It came to teach you a simple life lesson about these facts about which I speak to you now. You felt it instinctively at the time. Did you not, Joshua?"

Joshua replied, "Yes, I did. I did, but, then after a time I started to doubt with my mind and thought it was only a coincidence."

Papa Luca said, "That is what the mind always tries to do. If you let it, Joshua. The key is not to let the mind control you, or your thoughts. You must learn to listen to your heart. Your feelings and to the still small voice within you. Always, let that be your guide, if you can Joshua."

With that Papa Luca made his excuses and left. Joshua, only left with his pot of tea for company, sipped his tea and thought about all the things Papa Luca had just told him, and about how strange and yet familiar Papa Luca seemed to him!

***

The next morning Joshua woke up earlier than usual. He got dressed and then as quickly as he could he walked down to the beach near his house. It was only a mile or so and the country lane leading there was a beautiful tree lined path, following a rocky stream through the lush valley down to the ocean. Many times, Joshua, had reflected during this walk about all the other people who might have used it in centuries passed, to reach the old sea-harbour, which was once one of the busiest in the land and about the tales of the smugglers carrying illicit contraband on horseback along the narrow rocky path and riverbank from the sea to the village further inland.

When Joshua reached the harbour there he saw his old friend Harry, mending his fishing nets, lobster pots and staring at the sky, as if he was checking just what the weather held in store for the day.

Harry saw Joshua and greeted him warmly with a smile and the usual glint in his eye.

"You're not expecting me to take you dolphin spotting today, are you Joshua? Because I am going to be busy fishing today! That is if the dolphin has left a few for me to catch?" Said Harry with a wry smile.

"No, not at all. I am only out for a walk to collect my thoughts today. How are you doing anyway, Harry?" replied Joshua.

"Fine, just a bit tired. I spent much of the night worrying about stuff," replied Harry.

"I didn't think you were a worrier. What sort of stuff?" Joshua enquired.

"Personal stuff, mainly," replied Harry.

"But, also the state of the world. Global warming and how it is affecting so much of the planet right now," he continued,

"What are your thoughts on the situation Joshua?"

"What do you mean, global warming and its effect on the planet and stuff?" replied Joshua.

"Yes, all that stuff," said Harry.

"I don't know really, Harry. It is such a big issue. But, in the main I think every single country leader in the world needs to attend a long conference to make a united decision to make primarily the burning of fossil fuels illegal around the world and that the richer countries should pay the poorer countries to help them develop their own economies to build them without the need for fossil fuels. Also, to ban all single use plastic and phase out other plastics as much as feasibly possible," replied Joshua.

"That would be great if all the leaders of the different countries in the world could do that. Anyway, in the mean time I am just going to have to live in the moment and worry as little as possible by keeping busy," said Harry.

"Yes, keep busy and try not to worry. We all know that worrying doesn't do any good. Does it Harry?" replied Joshua.

"Too right. I have got enough to worry about just keeping my boat ship-shape!" replied Harry.

"Quite right," said Joshua. He continued his walk, leaving harry to attend to his fishing nets and walked along the sea-shore. The wind was starting to pick up he noticed and he could sense a storm in the air. The tide was full and the crest of the waves were being blown by the wind in a white trail along their tops into a fine sea spray. He watched the seagulls swoop down to the water's surface collecting bits of food and saw a cormorant flying in a straight line a few feet above the waves back towards land from its own fishing expedition, which he often witnessed when he was stood by the shore.

***

Joshua, had struggled for with anxiety since being a child, and he remembered that it was always just below the surface waiting to appear with each new challenge. He did not realise then what a handicap it was to his life and how it made it more difficult to manifest the things which he desired to have in his life. Only once being older did he have sufficient maturity to realise that anxiety was a common trait in many people's character. He often wondered what it would be like to live life worry free and what a blessing that would be and how much easier it would be to achieve the things in life that he had always wanted to achieve!

He remembered how, when he was a very young boy he would fear his father's response even over such minor events as getting wet feet while out playing, or fearing being asked to stand up and read out aloud in class at school. He reflected on how his anxiety had followed him 'like a thief in the night' – seemingly with the ongoing intention of trying to steal his peace of mind whenever the opportunity arose.

As Joshua had grown in years and his maturity developed, he had learnt various techniques to cope with these types of emotions. He had learnt to meditate as a young man to help calm his mind when times of fear and anxiety would trouble his own mind and emotions. Sitting in silence to face his own inner demons he found challenging but deeply rewarding and meditation had helped his growth in many ways and had helped to deepen his own spiritual awareness.

***

Joshua was sat in his favourite haunt – The Lion Hotel and looking out at the busy street. The seventeenth century hotel had been the resting place for many travellers over the period it had been standing. Joshua stared out of the wooden-sash window opened enough to allow a slight breeze to enter the room. The noise of the traffic seeped in to his private space and the sun shone outside. The pavements were now quieter after the summer visitors had vacated the holiday resort due to the approach of autumn. The town felt as if once again it had been handed back to him!

Joshua was revisiting a memory of an adventure a few years earlier in his own life, when a sudden bereavement in his own family had occurred and had left him feeling adrift and alone in the ocean of life's events and which are dealt to all.

A few days later having thought that he had spent more than enough time reflecting on the pain of his personal situation, Joshua found himself entering the local travel agency shop.

"Hello, how can I help you?" said the female travel agent and whom, Joshua knew to be the owner of the business.

Joshua replied, "I have decided to visit a small place in the Western Ghats, a mountain range in Southern India. I am planning a trip to visit a special guru there called Swami Baba. I feel that I need some answers to help me through a difficult time which I am going through right now. I just need your help with arranging the flights to get to my destination, I can sort out the accommodation when I arrive."

"Of course. I can help to make those arrangements," said the travel agent kindly with a smile.

"Yes, thank you. These things happen I guess. I have decided to use up all my leave for the year from my job for this year. I want to try and see the trip as an adventure, despite how I feel right now," replied Joshua.

"Quite right. Let's get on and make the arrangements for you flights to India, when do want to visit?" said the travel agent.

Joshua replied, "Early April - for three weeks!"

***

Joshua's flight touched down after an exhausting ten-hour flight at Mumbai airport in India. It was midnight by the time Joshua had passed through passport control. Upon leaving the exit terminal with his heavy rucksack with his few belongings required for his journey upon his back, he was immediately struck by the heat and humidity of the night air. Joshua felt quite vulnerable because he did not like being out of his comfort zone. For him this was a million miles out of it!

This was his first visit alone, so far from home and his first visit to this great, mystical and colourful land. He immediately noticed the poverty before even leaving the airport terminal. He saw several homeless people, even sleeping in the airports exit, where mosquitoes were dancing in the heavy sultry air in the street lights shadow. Joshua, wearily climbed light-headed with tiredness into the old Oxford Morris taxi, "Can you take me to the airport for the internal flights to Chennai, please?" Joshua said to the taxi driver, hoping that nearly all Indian people would perhaps be able to speak some English having once been a part of the British Empire.

"Okay," the taxi driver simply replied. They set off across the sprawling city into the night, eventually arriving at the airport. Joshua, was trying to keep his eyes open, despite the fact he was seeing sights new to his eyes, which he always found interesting, he fell asleep in the taxi, resting his weary head on his tatty old green canvas rucksack.

***

After a confusing initial arrival at the internal flights airport and having had a chance to catch up on some sleep in the departure lounge, prior to his next onward flight to the city of Chennai and formerly known as Madras, Joshua was feeling in better shape for his onward journey. On his flight to Chennai Joshua had his first conversation with an Indian couple, whom he was sat beside on his flight from one side of the vast country to the other.

"Where are you going, sir?" The man sat beside Joshua enquired. His wife sat beside him, smiling and awaiting Joshua's reply, too.

"I am on my first visit to India. I am here to visit a special man in the Western Ghats Mountains, in the south of India – a spiritual teacher called Swami Baba. I am hoping that he can teach me about some of the mysteries of life!" replied Joshua.

"Oh, okay, very nice," said the male passenger smiling and shaking his head side to side as he spoke in that inimitable Indian gesture of acknowledgement and understanding.

"Where are you going?" Joshua enquired.

"We are going to my brother's wedding in Chennai," the man replied.

"Oh, very nice," said Joshua, still light headed with exhaustion from so much travelling and still too tired to want to engage in further conversation with the couple sat beside him and so he turned to the aeroplanes small window beside him and tried to catch a few more glimpses of 'Old Bombay', as the planes wheels left the ground and soon soaring above the fringes of Mumbai.

Several hours later, Joshua's flight touched down in Chennai. He collected his rucksack from the luggage carousel and went to a waiting room at the airport's terminal entrance point to try to seek information about his second internal flight, which was to Madurai, further south of the country. Joshua spoke to the man on the check-in desk and said, "I have a ticket for the 12.30 pm flight to Madurai," still tired from his journey so far.

The man behind the desk smiled and shook his head, and replied, "Sorry, sir, that flight went early, an hour ago!"

"What do you mean the flight left early?" Joshua said, angrily and bewildered.

"You are now in India. It happens!" The desk attendant replied briskly.

Joshua felt anxious, as he was desperate to reach his destination.

"When is the next flight from here to Madurai then?" Joshua asked the desk attendant?"

"In three days, sir," he replied.

Joshua said nothing, instead he walked away from the check in desk and sat down in a waiting area in the airport lounge and started to pray!

***

After ten minutes or so, Joshua looked up and saw opposite him and a few feet away from where he was sat a taxi-booking booth. He knew it was about four hundred miles further to his destination – a small foothill station near the bottom tip of southern India. A place where the British Colonialists, earlier in the nineteenth century sought refuge from the intense heat of the summer and to seek some respite from the often forty-five degrees' centigrade summer temperatures of the area. Joshua, was eager already to seek refuge from the heat and he had only just arrived in the country.

Joshua, walked over to the man at the taxi-desk. He was about thirty years of age and the same sort of age as Joshua himself. Joshua anxiously looked at the man and said, "Is it possible to get a taxi from here to the foothill station called Kodaikanal, in the Southern Ghats Mountain range from you? I know it is a long way."

The man looked at Joshua for a few seconds hesitantly, before he replied,

"No, too far, sorry, sorry," he replied.

Joshua, went back to his seat forlornly.

A few moments later the same man walked back over to Joshua and said, "Yes, okay I will do it for eight-thousand rupees and there will be two drivers."

"Okay," replied Joshua relieved.

"Follow me," said the taxi-driver.

***

Joshua, and the taxi-driver walked out of the airport and by this time, Joshua was even more weary with tiredness after many hours of flying so far from home. His large old green backpack weighing him down further. Joshua, had made sure he looked the taxi-driver clearly in the eyes, to see if he felt he could trust him and that he would drive him to the old Kodaikanal foothill station so many miles away.

"The taxi will have A.C. (air-conditioning) due to the agreed price," said the taxi-driver. Joshua trusted his instincts, he could see a kindness in the man's eyes and he could feel in his own heart that the taxi-driver was a good man. He decided to trust him.

The man took Joshua to a small fifty cc motorcycle that the taxi-driver kept at the airport parking lot.

He said to Joshua, "Get on and hold on tight."

With his rucksack still on his back, Joshua climbed on board the small motorcycle and was taken to a humble tin roofed house on the edge of the city. Joshua, was aware of the risk he was taking, but surrendered to trusting in his instincts. At the house, they collected the taxi-drivers friend, who would be the second driver, due to the distance to be travelled. The second driver being about twenty-five years of age and a friend of the main driver. All three got into the a nineteen-sixties Morris Oxford taxi, with basic A.C. and set off on their long journey with Joshua resting his head on his rucksack as a pillow on the backseat exhausted.

***

The Journey of many hundreds of miles was mostly on narrow dirt roads with much traffic for most of the journey. Joshua's taxi driver, like the drivers of all the other vehicles on the road travelling in both directions, seemed to Joshua, to be constantly beeping their horns to make sure that the driver of the vehicle in front of them was aware of yet another risky overtake manoeuvre occurring.

Joshua, was by now delirious with tiredness from his time spent travelling and so little sleep – all he could do was to surrender his fears of being involved in a collision, to once again accept, that if this journey was to be his last, then so be it! At the same time the taxi would overtake time and again, only it seemed to Joshua, just in time to get out of the way before a large lorry passed them going in the opposite direction and having narrowly avoided a collision and leaving a trail of dust in its wake.

Occasionally, along the way, Joshua would awaken on the journey, yet soon fall back to sleep but when he was awake, alone on the back seat with both drivers sat up front, he was silent as they spoke very little English.

The taxi passed through one similar shanty village after another, children and adults mostly barefoot going about their daily business on the dry dusty dirt roads, while 'sacred' cows and bullocks wandered freely on the narrow dirt roads oblivious to the traffic and the searing heat. Joshua, had never travelled so far in his life-time and he didn't just feel out of his own comfort zone, but as if he was on some mysterious planet, simply because it was so different to what he was used to and having never visited such a country before. Yet, despite this to Joshua, it also had a strange familiarity that he could not quite fathom, he fell back asleep his head resting on his backpack filled with his few possessions for his unknown adventure.

Joshua, woke up and looked out of the taxi's window into darkness. He was aware of the cooler air and that the taxi was travelling uphill into the mountains at the southern tip of the country. The taxi trundled passed a sign for a town called 'Ooty' – another foothill station which he knew was close to his destination.

"Can you take me to a hotel on arrival in Kodaikanal please?" Joshua said.

"Yes, yes," said the driver.

It was midnight by the time the taxi pulled up outside a hotel. Joshua, thanked the two drivers and paid them the agreed eight thousand rupees' taxi fare at the doorstep of the hotel and which looked quite modern to Joshua's eyes and better than he had expected, the interior being decorated with a lot of white marble flecked stone, so it felt cool inside. He was shown to his room and was asleep in seconds.

***

The next morning, Joshua woke up after a good night's sleep. He felt a bit bewildered in his new surroundings and was still tired from his time spent travelling and as a result had not been able to take in as much as he had hoped on his journey up the mountain.

Kodaikanal, had changed over the years into a small holiday resort to which many visitors came for the cooler temperatures to escape the baking heat of the plains down below at sea level.

Joshua, did his morning meditation and then sorted out the clothes that he had brought with him inside his backpack. His journey to India was primarily to visit the Indian Swami-Baba, to help Joshua seek some answers to some of life's mysteries. He looked out of his rooms balcony, all he could see were a few green trees and some shops on the edge of the small town of the resort area.

Joshua, had first heard about Swami-Baba, when he was given a book about him by a woman he had met at a spiritual evening get together in his own home town, several years earlier. He had avidly read the book and hoped one day that he would find the chance to visit India and the famous Swami-Baba, who by the time of his visit was in his seventies and was slight in stature, standing only about five feet two inches tall, with a frizzy full head of black hair. He always wore a thin robe coloured usually in orange, white or yellow and which would reach down to his ankles. He went barefoot everywhere and generally did so without any trappings of wealth or privilege.

Joshua, was anxious still being so far out of his comfort zone once again, suffering with his own often crippling anxiety. He thought to himself that - it had taken him all his courage to make this journey alone! However, he was determined to face his own fears whatever the cost in terms of his own mental and emotional discomfort. Joshua, wanted to grow in his mind, body and spirit, he thought to himself. That had always been his desire; his intention to expand his mind and consciousness, to help him to learn who he really was and what his purpose was, being on Earth at this time of great change.

***

Joshua, decided to get his breakfast, not in his hotel but instead somewhere outside in the small town. The food was alien to him being so far from home. The day was bright and clear and although still tired from all his travelling, he decided to find a small café somewhere nearby.

After a short walk into town, he was struck firstly by the colourful dresses that the Indian women wore as they went about their business and with many also wearing beautiful garlands of flowers in their hair. Most of the people he saw were walking barefoot and the men were in the main dressed all in white loose cotton clothing. The people he passed smiled and he was immediately struck by their warmth and friendliness and he smiled to himself how they shook their heads quickly side to side as he witnessed people speaking often to one another, this being a common Indian gesture amongst many.

Joshua, found a café and sat outside and ordered a sweet tea called 'chai' and some toast. He paid the bill, a few rupees. He was struck by the low prices compared to back home in England and continued onwards to find the ashram where devotees of Swami-Baba would go whilst visiting the town. After a short time of walking along a road next to a large lake with many colourful white lotus flowers floating amongst their large green leaves on the lakes surface he saw a group of four men, two of whom were white skinned and they appeared to be of western origin, so, he said to one of them – a large and amiable looking man with long dark hair and a beard, "Excuse me, do you speak English?"

The man replied, "Yes, I do."

Joshua replied, "Oh, good. I am looking for Swami-Baba's ashram. Do you know where it is please?"

To which the man replied, "Yes, we do actually! We are all going there too. Some of us have been here a few days and are attending the ashram each day to see and listen to Swami-Baba. You can join us if you like. Are you on your own? My name is John. What is yours?"

He replied, "My name is Joshua, I would love to join you and as you are here for the same reason as myself, to listen to Baba's teachings. I only arrived late last night all the way from England. I still feel exhausted after my long journey."

John replied, I have come from the UK too, but I have been here a couple of days. You are most welcome to join our group. Are you from Bournemouth by any chance?"

Joshua replied, "I used to live there for many years."

John replied, "Yes, I think I recognise you from a spiritual talk I once went to at a hall there a few years ago."

Joshua replied, "Now you mention it, you look very familiar to me too. I think I recognise you as well. How strange is that and how weird – all this way from home. What are the chances?"

John replied, "Everything happens for a reason!" smiling as he spoke to Joshua.

Joshua replied, "Yes, I think you are quite right John."

John proceeded to introduce Joshua to the rest of the group of men with him, as it turned out each man had made the journey alone from their own respective homelands.

John said, "This is Puvan, he is from South Africa."

Joshua shook his hand, he looked Indian, was tall with a beard and he turned out to be much younger than his appearance suggested. He was what many people would call an 'old soul' but in a young person's body. He was twenty-seven years of age and on his second visit to India to see Swami-Baba. John then introduced Joshua to Mahesh, a slightly built Indian man from Delhi. Mahesh was quieter, more introverted than the other two men but he had a calmness and a goodness exuded from his being.

"We are on our way to the ashram now," said John.

Joshua, smiled with relief. He was no longer on his own, thousands of miles from home and he knew he was already on the right path and being looked after somehow!

***

Joshua, stayed in the same hotel for the first week of his three-week pilgrimage to India. One morning sat outside the same café, where he had drunk his tea and eaten his toast on the first morning, he saw sat there a man about eighty years in age. He had long grey hair and a long grey beard and was wearing a white gown, he carried a black walking stick with a golden handle. The man smiled over at Joshua and spoke to him, "What is your name young man?" The elderly man spoke with a distinct American accent.

"My name is Joshua," he replied to the elderly man sat near to him.

"And, my name is Albert. I am pleased to meet you, young man. I have seen you I think, in Swami's ashram. Am I not right?" The elderly man enquired.

"Yes, you are right but I have only just arrived. Yesterday, was my first visit to the ashram," replied Joshua.

"Really. I have been coming to visit Swami from the states for the last thirty years or so. What are your first impressions of Swami?" the man enquired.

Joshua replied, "I knew as soon as I saw Swami-Baba, that he was not an ordinary mortal. Not a normal human being."

"Yes, I agree. Swami, is said to be a Cosmic Avatar. If you think of Jesus, as being a Planetary Avatar, a Cosmic one is just that "Cosmic'," replied the elderly man sipping his expresso coffee. The sun shone brightly and the heat was rising. It was barely eight in the morning and Joshua was already contemplating finding some shade. He had never known such a fierce sun. He was after all a person from the northern hemisphere, an often cold, dark land that England is rightly known as and for much of the year.

"What is an Avatar exactly then?" Joshua enquired, wrinkling his nose as he spoke to the elderly American. He could sense he was a special man and with a life's catalogue of interesting experiences which Joshua would love to hear in one sitting with the mysterious man if possible.

"An Avatar, is a being with the full awareness that he is him or herself a divine incarnation of the wisdom and full power that the energy of God possesses," replied the man.

"Really, what does that mean exactly? For I cannot comprehend such a person. Is that really true?" replied Joshua.

"Yes, it is true," replied the man. He continued on, "For you are very privileged to be here now, for Swami will not live many more years. He is almost my age and I am eighty-one years of age. In the nineteen-forties I was a Broadway dancer you know. But that was long ago!"

The American paused for a while as he appeared to reflect on his memories of the past. Then he continued to speak, he spoke softly with a quite assurance and said, "Many native people of this country want to visit Swami, but unless he permits it on the highest level, even those from nearby will be unable to visit him. Events in their own life will preclude such a visit for whatever reason you might possibly think of, illness, work, family commitments, money, do you know what I mean?"

"Yes," replied Joshua. The man continued, "I can tell from your accent that you are English, am I not right?"

"Yes," replied Joshua. The man continued to speak, "Swami's message is simple. All are of God, and all beings and in fact all of creation in the entire universe is divine. All are connected. To use a cliché, all are 'one'. That is the essence of his teaching. You will discover that even if you have not done so already, my young friend. How old are you, young man? I would say perhaps, thirty years, correct?"

"Yes, you are exactly right. I am thirty years old now," replied Joshua.

"Young man, you have many years ahead of you yet to live. You will have many adventures ahead and I hope you find what you are seeking and I must go now. I have things to do. Nice to meet you," said the elderly American. He stood up using his black walking stick for support, his dark brown eyes penetrated deeply into Joshua's own eyes, as he shook his hand and Joshua bid him farewell.

Joshua, remained at the café, sitting for a little while longer and reflecting on the American's words. He imagined the man to be a bit of a 'guru' or teacher in his own right and someone, Joshua had always wished to encounter, but never thought he had at the time. He reflected that already he was to be further in the company of Swami-Baba the Cosmic Avatar. He could not really comprehend the fullness, the reality, the significance of his good fortune to be in Kodaikanal and in India at that time, at least not until many years later in his own future life.

Joshua, continued to sit at the table outside the café. He tried to imagine for a moment, Swami sat opposite him at the next table, staring and smiling at him. Then instead, he imagined Jesus sat opposite him and in the clothes that Jesus would have worn two-thousand years ago. For a moment, Joshua wished they could be sat opposite him in that moment and then for just an instant a truth dawned on him: he realised that any person sat in front of him, at any time, would be God in human form, but that very few people were yet awake to the fact – that, that is who they truly are!

***

The next day Joshua was up at four a.m. The plan was to meet his new friends, John, Mahesh and Puvan outside the gates of Swami-Baba's ashram.

Swami, most years, though not all, would visit the ashram in Kodaikanal in April to escape the higher temperatures of the plains below, the old hill station being situated at 2,133 metres above sea-level was to add to its beauty also surrounded by thick shola forests, flowery meadows and grasslands.

Joshua, walked the mile along the road from his hotel to the ashram passed the large picturesque lake and along a shady-tree lined road. On arrival at the ashram gates, he saw his friends waiting for him sat on the roadside patiently at the side of the gates – the women were lined up separately on the other side of the entrance gates as men and woman were kept separate for these spiritual gatherings to see Swami and while listening to his talks or discourses as they were often referred to. It was tradition there to wear loose white cotton clothing – rather like pyjamas and Joshua had invested in a couple of pairs of them on his arrival, as they were inexpensive compared the prices back home.

John, greeted him and said, "We have come early. We will be here until about six a.m. when the sevadals will come to us and hold out a cloth bag, from which we must choose a coloured token and then we will be let into the ashram in a certain order according to the colour of the token we have picked. This is to prevent people who get here the earliest from always getting in first and therefore always getting the best seat in the ashram and get the closest to where Swami sits."

Joshua replied, "What is the point of getting here early then?"

John laughed and replied, "True, but that is just what people do, hoping to see Swami I suppose!"

Mahesh and Puvan, were already sat cross-legged in the line at the roadside patiently meditating. As they spoke, they were approached by a young local man with a bicycle selling chai-tea.

"Chai, chai," shouted the young male street seller. He carried a tea-urn strapped to each side of his old bicycle. Chai, being a sweet Indian tea and infused with other various herbs. John and Joshua purchased a cup of the sweet tea for a few rupees and sipped it to help them wake up. Though it was early and they were many meters above sea level, the temperature was still a very pleasant twenty degrees centigrade and would not usually go above twenty-five degrees centigrade at that time of year.

The sevadals, who also acted like security guards and to help serve the many visitors from around the world who had come to visit Swami, approached John and Joshua and held out the cloth-bag in front of them holding the tokens as they were still sat in line outside the ashram gates.

"I have got blue," said John.

"Blue too," said Joshua.

Soon after one of the sevadals shouted, "Blue is first," to the men waiting outside the gates patiently in one line. John and Joshua quickly walked through the open gates and up the drive and into the grand house to a large room which was like a small hall inside. At the end of the hall was a single large gold coloured chair upholstered with a crimson coloured velvet.

John and Joshua sat on the floor near to the front of the large golden chair, while the rest of the so called 'devotees', filed into the hall of the large resplendent white house in which Swami stayed and where he spent time teaching his devotees.

Joshua looked at John and said, "This is all a bit like a dream don't you think. What happens now?"

"I don't know," John replied with a whisper.

***

It was Easter Friday in April that John and Joshua found themselves sat on the floor like two junior school children in a hall filled now with some of Swami's many devotees from all around the world. Some of the audience at the front of the small crowd of about two-hundred people started to sing a devotional song or bhajans, as they are known in India and with verses often repeated in the most melodious of ways.

During this time, Swami emerged from a door at the front of the audience and sat on the golden chair. He was diminutive in size with thick dark bushy hair and wearing a thin orange cotton robe, the length of which reached his ankles almost covering his bare feet from view. He was accompanied by an elderly Indian gentleman who stood beside him and was an interpreter for Swami's words which were spoken in one of the many Indian languages, called 'Telegu'. His words were translated into English by the interpreter to help most of the audience understand what he was saying to them. Swami, spoke at length on various spiritual topics, followed by some bhajans. Swami, started to join in with the song, which he must have sung so many times and his voice was like nectar to the ears and the soft lilting tones of his voice captured the attention of the audience.

As Joshua looked at the top of Swami's head, he noticed a haze around it just like something you see sometimes above the surface of a road in the distance on a hot summers day. As he continued to stare at it, he doubted what his own eyes were showing him – as he had never seen such a thing around another person, as Joshua continued to doubt what his eyes were seeing, the haze around Swami's head started to spread out further and further until it finally filled the room. Then suddenly, to Joshua's eyes at least the haze shot back in an instant to once again only extend just a few inches above Swami's hairline, as it had first appeared to him.

Joshua thought that this event had occurred as if to silence his own doubt about whether what he was seeing was real, or imagined.

Swami, Joshua realised from early on, was by no means an ordinary mortal – "Love All. Serve All," was one of his mantra's and a big part of Swami's teaching to all those who came to see him. "You are not the body, not the mind. You are consciousness," he would repeat this phrase often to those present at his talks.

Joshua, John and the rest of the audience sat listening intently to the words of the small Indian man, with the mop of black frizzy hair, sat on the golden chair in his thin cotton orange robe. He wore no jewellery, no watch or shoes. He lived a simple life and had lived this way for the seventy or so years since his birth into a poor family in India. There were tales of him picking fruits from trees when he was just a child himself and then transforming them in to sweets for his young friends. This being, just one of the many tales that followed him.

As the Easter talk ended and as Swami left the room when the bhajan singing subsided, a whisper began to fill the room and one by one each person present in the hall became aware and looked closely at a timely image which had magically and mysteriously appeared in the velvet material on the front of the upright section of the golden chair which Swami had been sat on until a few moments previous, there had appeared clearly a picture of the face of Jesus!

***

Joshua, exited the ashram with his friends all of whom were excited by what they had just seen and chatted about it as they walked. Outside the ashram, they turned left along the large Kodaikanal lake covered with the flowering white water-lily's and stopped at a café alongside the lake where they each ordered themselves a refreshing cool drink.

Joshua said to his friends, "The picture of the face of Jesus, in the velvet backed chair Swami was sat on – it appeared as if by magic. Have any of you seen Swami perform any other miracles, like that before?"

Puvan, paused and then replied, "Yes, I have seen him manifest many different things for his devotees who come here and at his main ashram in Puttaparthi near

Bangalore, where I have visited him. He often also manifests a sacred ash called vibuti – it just appears from his hands and he gives it to people, it has magical healing qualities. I have seen him many times manifest from thin air, various trinkets and pieces of jewellery for devotees, sometimes very valuable ones I might add, and give it to them! He literally pulls such things out of thin air!" Puvan paused from speaking for a moment then continued to tell of one such incident that he witnessed.

"I once met an Italian man, for whom Swami manifested one million Lira! He gave it to him and said to the man that he, the man in question had been St. Francis of Assisi in a previous life-time and that God had owed him the money!"

Joshua replied, "These are incredible stories. Most people would just not believe that sort of stuff, saying instead it was just lies or trickery. What do you think about it all Puvan?"

"I believe totally, sometimes even if I have not seen it always with my own eyes," replied Puvan, with a stern expression on his face.

"I have been a devotee of Swami for many years, and though I am still young, I know that each of us is here for a reason and we are all very privileged to be here and many would like to be in our place. Perhaps, it is for what we have already done in a previous life-time or simply what our destiny holds for us in the future. What do you think of it all?" Puvan, said to Joshua.

Joshua, paused for a moment, to reflect before answering Puvan's question, "I am not sure. I know already that Swami is not an ordinary human being. This is all a very surreal experience for me being here, from the moment I met John, who recognised me soon after I arrived, I knew then that some sort of magic had brought me to this place. It makes my life right now feel much more mysterious and interesting than usual I suppose!"

Joshua continued, "Do you think Swami is God, Puvan? You know, someone like Jesus?"

"I think Swami is an incarnation of God in human form and with the full knowledge of who he really is and the power that he has at his disposal. That is why he can perform such miracles." Puvan replied with a twinkle in his eyes as he finished answering Joshua's question. Joshua was aware of Puvan's unusual degree of wisdom for his age and a little younger than Joshua himself.

The group of friends continued to drink their cool refreshing drinks and reflecting on what had just been said and enjoying the cool breeze as it blew out across the lake as they sat in the shade of the large trees.

***

The next morning the friends were up once again bright and early and in the men's line waiting to enter the ashram, by which time morning light had arrived for the start of a new day. They each ordered a cup of chai tea from the chai-seller carrying the urns of tea on his bicycle.

Each friend chose a token from the cloth bag presented by the sevadal and even though the friends had been amongst the first to arrive and take their positions in the men's queue outside the ashram gate, all but Puvan had chosen a token which meant they should enter the ashram last. This only bothered them because it meant sitting outside of the hall and that they would not be getting a view of Swami until after he exited the hall after giving his spiritual discourse or talk.

John, Mahesh and Joshua were each guided by the sevadals to sit in the outside courtyard next to the house. As usual it was another beautiful and dry day, so that the weather was not an issue. They would have to wait up to an hour sat on the concrete floor, until Swami made his appearance, but for this reason many carried meditation seats to make themselves more comfortable. Sitting outside however, meant that there was a scramble by the crowd to sit nearest to a clear space left for Swami to walk through the audience of devotees. He would do this to take letters from some of them near to where he passed by, or to allow those that wished to touch his feet and thereby receive a blessing known as Padamaska, might be bestowed upon them, so that whoever received such good fortune, to be able to be sat close enough to Swami as he passed by were able to reach out and touch his feet.

On this day, Joshua found himself three rows back from the path space left for Swami to walk passed the audience. Joshua, had written a letter before he departed on his journey to India, asking for his deepest wishes to be answered and in the hope, such an occasion would occur for him to have such an opportunity. However, he knew being three rows back could prevent this from happening.

Suddenly Joshua noticed Albert, the elderly American man whom he had met previously at the café nearby. He smiled kindly at Joshua and said, "Hello my friend would you like to sit in my place at the front? I have had the good fortune to do so many times before, so it is okay if you want to sit here to get close to Swami."

Joshua beamed back happily at Albert and replied, "Yes please, that is so kind. The elderly man and Joshua swapped places and Joshua sat cross-legged on the floor and waited for Swami to appear outside, he turned to smile back at Albert and whisper "Thank you".

After about an hour of waiting patiently, Swami appeared from the adjacent building. Excitement filled the air amongst the devotees and John who had also got a space at the front, waited with anticipation for Swami to arrive, so that they could receive padamaska and hopefully to give any letters they had with them to Swami, wishing for the fulfilment of their deepest wishes whether for themselves or others!

As swami drew level with where Joshua was sitting upon the ground, he did not look at him but Joshua took the chance to gently touch Swami's small bare feet very fleetingly as he passed by. A warm smile enveloped Joshua's being and he felt lucky to have such an opportunity. He briefly wondered how it might affect his life in the future, or if at all! A few moments later he also managed to give Swami his own letter, which he simply passed to a sevadal walking beside him, who's task was to carry the many letters accepted by Swami from the various devotees. Suddenly, Joshua and John noticed one elderly male devotee hand over a letter to Swami. No sooner had Swami taken the letter, then they saw Swami in an instant throw the letter back at the devotee. Those in the crowd who were watching noticed the letter in mid-air crushed into a ball by some invisible force and it fell to the ground. A silent hush enveloped all those present for a few moments followed by much enthusiastic comments by the many devotees present on what they had just witnessed. Swami serenely moved on taking and accepting letters from more devotees.

John turned to Joshua and said, "The letter must have had something bad written inside."

Joshua nodded back in agreement and said, "Yes, I think you are right! I couldn't believe what I saw. The letter was just crushed into a ball in mid-air, as if by magic wasn't it!"

As Swami walked away down the cleared space between the devotees, Joshua noticed once again the halo around Swami's head. He stared perplexed by it as it appeared as before, just like the haze above the tarmac of a road on a hot summers day. The halo was always there visible at least to Joshua's eyes and with Swami wherever he went. A sudden screech pierced the silence, Joshua turned and noticed a couple of the small native monkeys on an adjacent wall seemingly arguing over a piece of rotten fruit that one of them had found. The smaller monkey snatched the piece of fruit out of the larger grey monkey's hand and was pursing the fruit prize-winner along the top of a nearby wall.

Joshua smiled to himself, he felt fortunate and happy to be in India. He was settling into his new environment and looked forward to his stay at the Ashram for the next three weeks. He knew that he had many questions and was looking for the answers, just like many others present. He wondered if he was not the mind, not the body, like Swami taught the devotees, but in fact consciousness, but what did that really mean in a world full of challenges and often one full of pain for so many? He paused for a moment in his thoughts, 'maybe it was just acceptance - acceptance of whatever life throws at each of us in each moment!'

Everyone who visited soon realised that there was a hierarchy of expectation whenever devotees or spiritual seekers visited the place that Swami was visiting at the same time. Most of the people around the world who followed his teachings wished for an interview with this 'Avatar' and Joshua was no different, even though

Swami would often say – inner-view, not interview: meaning look at oneself, look within at our own faults and try to fix them as best we can.

Joshua would often reflect on his own weakness's and limitation but not necessarily his own faults as such. He knew he had an anxious disposition and so was prone to worry rather often. Joshua, suffered from some irrational fears too, and was keen to escape them and move to a greater level of mental peace and freedom from such thoughts which often troubled him.

One of the things many devotees wished for as well as a private one to one audience with Swami was something also more tangible!

***

The next day Joshua threw on his clothes after a quick shower, he got up so early, it was too early for breakfast at the hotel and so, once again found himself walking along the tree lined avenue next to the large lake only to reach the gates of the ashram and join his friends in the men's queue and for the day's address by Swami.

Puvan, John and Mahesh were already stood next to the front gates which were still firmly locked. Puvan said to John, "What are you hoping will happen today?"

speaking with his distinctive South African drawl, which Joshua was starting to get used to. John replied, "An interview would be nice to have, but I doubt I will get one!"

Puvan, stared at John for a moment and asked, "Why do you want an interview so much?"

John replied, "Because it would make me feel special I suppose, if I am really honest, Puvan!"

Puvan replied, "That is a very honest answer John. I respect you for saying that."

Puvan asked no further questions and went off to look for the chai-tea seller.

John said to Joshua, "We have a space at the bungalow that we are all renting. Do you want to join us? It will be much cheaper than staying at the hotel for the rest of your stay Joshua?"

Joshua replied, "Thanks John, that would be great. I like the hotel, but it is a bit lonely being on my own there. I have not made any friends there, so it would be nice to stay with you guys, especially as we have now got to know each other a bit."

By this time Puvan returned with some cups of chai tea for them all to drink. Mahesh and Puvan nodded as if to agree that it would be nice for Joshua to join them at the old small bungalow they were renting cheaply for their joint stay in the ashram town.

Soon the gates were unlocked, the group of friends, all in the same line that morning managed to get into the ashram's main building first, thereby acquiring good places to sit near to Swami's crimson velvet chair. Soon the bhajan singing started and filled the small hall with a feeling of divinity which was added to by the sweet smell of burning incense. Swami, appeared and sat on the large chair at the front of the hall, his usual interpreter stood beside him. Swami, joined in with the bhajan singing as he often did, his sweet soft tones adding to the special spiritual atmosphere present amongst the audience.

Swami gave a talk about trusting one's conscience and letting it be one's guide through life. Especially, in times of difficulty, indecision or confusion. He would say it is the voice of the soul or the spirit speaking to each person through their heart and that all should listen and know it as the captain of their own ship and to love all, serve all!

Joshua and his three friends were smiling throughout, imbibing the sweet nectar of the wisdom of

Swami's speech's as they did most day's and their brightness of being added to the quality of the atmosphere in the hall. So much so that Swami spotted the group of friends and at one point Swami seemed to point them out to his interpreter beside him.

Joshua and his friends noticed this and an excitement lit up the group. John said excitedly, "Did you see that, did you see Swami has pointed us out. Could it mean we are all going to go in to see Swami after the service for an interview each? I really hope we are, that would be amazing!"

Puvan, said in a calmer voice, "Maybe, maybe."

Joshua didn't say anything, he just looked and smiled at the rest of them with his fingers crossed. He knew that to be given an interview was special and rare!

***

Soon after, the audience in the hall could leave and as usual mostly westerners were inside. Those in the audience from India were generally not allowed into the hall. The reason often given, was because Swami knew most westerners visited him in the three weeks or so that he attended the Kodaikanal Ashram each year as it was cooler. The rest of the year, he was available to his native countrymen at his other main ashram near Bangalore and another one at his birthplace, a town called Puttaparthi, elsewhere in India and where the temperatures were always higher and less tolerable to the western devotees who made journeys often thousands of miles to visit him and just as John and Joshua had all the way from the United Kingdom.

On this day, before the group of friends left the hall, the interpreter said to the four friends, "Swami would be very happy if you could all see him shortly, after all the other audience members have left. You stay seated as you are by his seat and he will return to the hall and speak to you all together as he has told me. He will give you an interview!"

The friends, all looked at each other with a big smile on their faces. Each of them held the palms of their hands together next to their hearts in thanks for Swami's gesture of granting them an interview. They remained and sat silently awaiting Swami's return into the hall.

About five minutes later Swami came back in, he seemed to almost float above the wooden floor as he walked. As usual he wore only his orange robe which reached the ground and with the usual halo encircling the crown of his head. Joshua, stared at the halo as

Swami sat down on his chair. As he did so, he waived his hand in the air several times at waist height with his palm facing upwards, as if from nowhere, a fine gold chain appeared with a gold crucifix attached to it. It swung from Swami's fingers and the full length of the piece of jewellery was revealed to their eyes. He had manifested it from thin air and he gave it to Puvan, who reached out and took it bowing as he approached Swami and as he returned to sit in thanks for gift.

Swami said, through his interpreter, "Each of you of you has travelled a long way to meet me and you have each had much difficulty in your short lives until now, I know. This will change – for now the blessings of the divine will smooth out your paths to make your lives easier. You have each chosen many of your own difficulties, for one reason or another. But this was because you still had and still have much to learn in this life. You are all here now, because each of you has known each other at different times, in other lives. Nothing happens by coincidence. You are not all here now by coincidence, you are here to come together to heal. Not just now, but in the future also. The gift I give you is the assurance that I have just given to you all. You will all go your separate ways when you leave here but you will never forget your time here, however, for each it is different and for each of you it is special in a different way as each of you faces a new chapter here in your lives. When you leave remember God goes with you always. You are each a part of God and know that always in your heart and soul. Love all. Serve all."

Swami manifested from his hands some sacred vibuti powder and gave some to all four of the friends gathered in front of him. He placed his thumb and smeared some of the ash on the forehead of each of them. Then he rubbed his closed left hand with his right hand and a light came out of both hands as he did so. Then he opened his left hand and called Joshua over to him. Joshua moved humbly towards Swami, head bowed in respect. Swami, asked Joshua to hold out his right hand as Joshua did so he placed a gold ring on to Joshua's finger, the ring had a large green emerald in the centre and a Cobra's head facing each side of the stone and in the engraved head of each Cobra were several sparkling diamonds.

Joshua looked at the ring and said, "Thank you Swami, thank you."

With that Swami got out of the chair and left the room as gracefully as he had entered it a few minutes earlier.

***

The four friends each got up and walked out of the hall and down the driveway to the road beside the lake. Each was silent for a while, though they all had a smile on their face. They had been granted a group interview, maybe not quite so good as an individual interview, but rare all the same. They each felt especially blessed by a higher power and were chosen for whatever reason. In the past many famous individuals of all types, including royalty had tried to get an interview and failed. For some reason, Swami had given each of the friends his personal blessing and two had received gifts manifested by the 'Cosmic Avatar', someone like Jesus, Joshua thought to himself.

Joshua took from his finger the ring Swami had given to him, he looked at it closely deciding then that he would never sell it as it was priceless and would help him to remember always that life was also a gift – from spirit to all people. This ring would always be his own special reminder of his trip to India to meet Swami, a God-man, with a halo around his head, beyond that of ordinary figures of royalty and who only had a material halo crown of gold metal, but Swami had a halo of a supernatural essence of being. A being who Joshua believed, knew all that there was to know about everyone and everything.

'Why could Swami not speak English fluently then without the need of an interpreter?' Joshua thought to himself. He put the thought aside for the time and instead thought that maybe there was a good reason for that too!

***

The next morning Joshua awoke, it being his last night in his bed at the comfortable hotel and before moving in with his new friends into the humble bungalow for the rest of his stay in Kodaikanal for the extra company.

After Joshua woke up in the morning he remembered a dream that previous night about Swami. He had met Swami in the dream; he was out alone at night in a forest. Joshua, recalled saying to Swami in the dream, "Swami, is there anything that you cannot do? Is there any miracle that you cannot perform?"

Swami, pointed to the night sky and in perfect English, replied to Joshua's question and said, "Look up at the full moon in the sky my friend."

As Joshua did so, the moon simply vanished before his eyes. In the next instant Swami held out his right hand and opened his palm and there he held, emblazoned in light what appeared to be an exact replica of the moon itself, only for the fact that it was now shrunken down to the size of only a tennis ball. The miniature moon appeared to be hovering an inch or so above Swami's hand. Joshua, stretched out his hand to touch it.

Swami, quickly in response to this gesture said, "No, no, do not touch it, it would be very harmful to touch it now!"

In the next instant, the miniature moon disappeared from Swami's outstretched palm and magically reappeared in the night sky, as it had been only a minute previous.

Joshua, remembered no more of his dream. He paused and reflected while still in bed, on what the meaning of the dream might be. He concluded that perhaps it simply meant that there was no limit to the powers of the mysterious, Swami-Baba! Perhaps, also it meant that therefore there was no limit to God's powers either.

Joshua, had for much of his stay at the old hill-station town and during his visits to the ashram, especially during the periods of queuing with his friends and due to his single status kept an eye on the female visitors to the ashram, even though he knew that it did not feel quite right in such an environment. Joshua, it could not be denied enjoyed women's company a lot. However, he knew that for this adventure he had embarked upon to the other side of the world in rural India was not the right time or place to seek out romance or any sexual adventures with others. This trip was from the outset in Joshua's mind a sort of pilgrimage to discover aspects of his own nature and to heal some of his own pain concerning a relationship passed, for Joshua, had been married for a short period of time and even though he was in love with his wife, the marriage had failed and it had broken his heart. This trip for Joshua was in part to help him heal and recover from the deep upset he had felt from this relationships demise.

However, as much as Joshua tried to keep his focus on his spiritual intentions of his own progress concerning matters purely of the soul, his eyes and passions of the heart kept on distracting him from his spiritual focus.

One morning after the darshan or service, at the ashram and after everyone had filed out of the grounds of the building, Joshua walked back alongside the lake towards the town. He saw the attractive blonde haired woman, who had caught his eye on several mornings, while he was queuing for the darshan.

Joshua, approached the woman. She was about thirty years of age and she wore a fine green silk Sari, woven into its fabric, were gold and silver coloured threads. Joshua said to her, "Hello, I have seen you on several occasions, visiting Swami for darshan. Where are you from?" The attractive blonde haired woman looked at Joshua and smiled. Her eyes were bright green and she had very pale skin and stood only about five feet and three inches tall.

She replied, "Russia, my name is Claudia. What is your name?"

"My name is Joshua," he replied.

"Where are you from, Joshua?" asked the Russian woman.

"I am from England. I have come to visit Swami because I have recently heard about him being a person like Jesus. So, I had to come and find out for myself and to see if the things I had heard about him are true or not."

"And do you think that they are true?" The Russian woman replied.

"I think so, yes. I believe they are true. I can tell he is not an ordinary human being." Joshua replied.

"Would you like to join me for a drink by any chance?" Joshua asked her.

"Yes, that would be nice," said Claudia, with a distinct Russian sounding accent and continued, "I would very much like to do that."

Joshua smiled at her, "Great," he replied. Though, immediately thought to himself, 'how wise is this?' Was he there to meet a beautiful and mysterious foreign woman, or was he there, as his soul was telling him to look within his own self, as to why he searched for the love he desired, always from another, rather than trying to find it within his own-self.

Joshua pulled back a chair at the table outside the café, that he and his friends usually visited after the darshan. The elegant Russian woman said, "Thank you," and sat down.

"Would you mind getting me a lemonade? I am happy to pay," she said.

"No, I will pay," replied Joshua, and went to fetch some drinks for them both. Joshua returned with two bottles of cold lemonade and sat next to her. Joshua tried to not be flirtatious, as he might usually, on such an occasion since he was single and showing an interest as to why she was in India, he asked, "Why are you in India, might I ask?"

"I am here to seek spiritual answers to my own questions. I have many problems in my own life at home," the woman replied.

She offered the information freely and continued, "My boyfriend back home and who I live with, is in the Russian Mafia and I am not happy with this. It does not feel good to me, but I love him, so I stay. I have come here to seek answers about my way forward in this matter." The Russian woman, looked intense and concerned as she spoke, and as she did so, Joshua could not help but be transfixed by her beauty. He smiled back at her and said, "I too, am here with concerns of the heart. I have just suffered the break-up of a short but intense marriage. I am here to find some answers and hopefully some sign-posts about the best way forward to help me with the next stage of my own life too."

The Russian woman took out a packet of cigarettes from her shoulder bag and offered one to Joshua, "Would you like one?" she said.

"No, thank you, I don't smoke," replied Joshua.

"That is good, many people smoke and drink in my country. I think because so many people are miserable. Life is hard in Russia for many people and the weather is often terrible!" she said.

Joshua, looked deeply into her green eyes and thought to himself, that even though she was beautiful he could not help but detect an icy coldness in her eyes. He wondered if that alone, belied the fact as to how she could be in a relationship with someone in the Mafia, perhaps!

She continued, "I had heard about Swami-Baba. A friend visited him here two years ago and told me many stories which made me want to come here. She told me that Swami was like Jesus and I wanted to see if it was true."

"And what do you think? Do you think Swami is the return of Jesus Christ?" asked Joshua.

"I don't know yet! But he is different to everyone I have ever met and the way he produces things as if by magic, as gifts for people and such things. I saw him the other day throw back the letter which was crushed in mid-air as if by some mystical force. Were you there? Did you see it too?" she asked Joshua.

"Yes, I saw it happen too," Joshua replied.

She continued to speak, "So, I am here to decide if I am on the right path with my boyfriend and to discover if Swami is another Jesus person."

Joshua thought to himself as she spoke that she was used to living the high-life, at least by Russian standards. He could somehow tell that she was used to living in a world where money was not an issue.

"I hope you get the answers you seek," replied Joshua. At another time, Joshua might have thought of continuing his flirtation with such a beautiful woman but he knew that it was not the time or place. He also had enough sense to know that the girlfriend of a member of the Russian Mafia was no-go territory!

Joshua finished his drink and thanked her for their discussion and bid her farewell and set off back down the road and returned to his hotel. He packed up his few belongings into his green canvas rucksack and went in search of his friends, John, Puvan and Mahesh. He was looking forward to their company for the rest of his stay in Kodaikanal and at the bungalow that they shared and saving a few thousand rupees in the process, he would often tell himself, due to his own poverty consciousness, that 'he was not made of money, anyway!'

Joshua settled his bill in reception at his hotel where he had stayed since his arrival in the town. As he left the hotel he saw his three friends talking together nearby as they had left the ashram a bit later than him and had spent time looking at items for sale at the market near to the ashram's gates. They had been buying incense and other gifts for relatives and friends for their eventual return home.

John said, "Hey, Joshua it looks like you are ready to join us, we are just going to get something to eat so come and join us."

"Okay," replied Joshua. The four friends walked into the nearby town to find a restaurant, with a shaded outdoor eating area, where the food was not too expensive.

Each of them were still talking about their recent group interview with Swami and their good fortune to have received such an honour. Puvan, was also having difficulties with his marriage back in his home country it transpired and he was struggling to maintain the relationship. John, too had been divorced for several years and had no contact with his two teenage children which caused him much pain and suffering, due to a bitter divorce with his former wife. The only one of the four friends who had not yet it seemed suffered one of life's blows through relationship difficulty was Mahesh. His English, was not so good as Mahesh, it transpired, lived still with his mother in Bangalore, an up and coming high-tech modern city in central India. Mahesh, was always smiling and had a sweet and gentle nature like most of his fellow countrymen.

After their mixed dal and rice meal given to them on large green banana-tree leaves, used instead of plates, and cups of sweet tasting chai-tea, they paid their bill and walked back along the main road eventually reaching a dirt-track which went down a hill and reached a small, humble bungalow, where the four of them intended to sleep each night until their journey's back home.

Joshua, looked at the accommodation. It was a lot less luxurious than the four-star hotel he had just left. The cheapness compared to British prices would make it all the more bearable, Joshua thought to himself. He decided to treat the humble bungalow simply as another challenge and just be grateful for the company of his new-found friends and that he was no longer alone for now.

***

On the first evening that Joshua spent with Puvan, John and Mahesh in the bungalow, he had a chance to get to know his new friends better. They decided after so much walking and after another hot day to stay in together for the evening. Joshua asked Puvan, and who was the most knowledgeable out of the group about Swami's life story and his magical powers.

Joshua, said to Puvan, "How did Swami-Baba first become well known in India?"

Puvan replied, "Swami, was born in a small and poor village in central India. The story goes that the birth was like that of Jesus: a miraculous conception. Swami's mother on one particular day, saw a ball of light come towards her when she was out in the fields and it went inside her stomach and she subsequently became pregnant.

As a young child, Swami would pick fruit sometimes from tree's and turn the fruit in to sweets for his young friends. His powers grew as he got older and he left home as a young man as he felt a divine calling to set up an ashram in his home village. The ashram from tiny beginnings grew and over time he became more and more well-known and Swami eventually became famous not just in India but around the world. Each of us have our own reasons for being here."

Joshua, paused and turned to John, who was over six feet tall and built like a lumber-jack and lived in his own area of woodland back in England, he knew a lot about survival skills and had been on his own conscious spiritual path for some years by the time they met in India.

Joshua said to him, "John, how did you find out about Swami? Was there any particular story you heard about him which inspired you to come here to visit him?"

John, was sat cross-legged on the hard stone floor, except for a small piece of cloth that he used as a make-shift seat of little purpose and replied, "I heard a story about him first from a friend when I was visiting Glastonbury, in Somerset a few months ago. He had already been out to visit Swami last year and while in India he had met a man who was well known in the

United States, who had told him a story about something that happened to him, whereby his life was saved by Swami. He did not know who he was at the time!"

"What happened?" asked Joshua.

John continued with the story that had been relayed to him by the man in question,

"He told me that the man was one of the owners of a famous global chain of restaurants. One day he had been driving his sports car too fast around a bend in California. The car left the road and rolled down a sloping cliff, about a thousand feet. He said he should have died but that he was saved by a small Indian looking man in an orange coloured robe with a mop of curly black hair who had magically suddenly appeared inside his sports car next to him and who had wrapped himself around the man who was driving it to save him. When the car stopped rolling down the cliff-side he could emerge from the wrecked car alive and uninjured. The mysterious small Indian man had disappeared after the car came to a rest.

The driver of the sports car mentioned the incident to a friend and discovered that the mystery man who saved him was Swami-Baba. He started to visit Swami's ashram in India all the way from the United States. He went to visit him in India for over twelve years and Swami did not even look at him for all those years, let alone grant him an interview but eventually he did.

The man sold his shares in the famous restaurant chain for over one-hundred million dollars and with most of that money he had built, a super-speciality hospital, free for treatment to anyone in the world and near to Swami's main ashram in India. It was built in accordance with sacred geometry for the architectural design of the building and by a famous architect I believe."

Joshua replied, "Wow, what an amazing story. Do you believe it?"

"Yes, I do," replied John.

"Swami, has unlimited powers. He knows all and sees all. He is the full embodiment of God in a human form I do believe," said Puvan, who had been listening to John intently, as he had relayed the story to Joshua.

"Do you think he is God, then Puvan? Someone like Jesus," Joshua enquired.

"Yes, I do," replied Puvan.

"Have you seen Swami, also perform many miracles then Puvan?" asked Joshua.

"Yes, I have. As I have said before I believe also that his powers are unlimited. But he does not make things easy for those who come here hoping to be just fixed or healed. For karma is karma, and each must find their own path to peace and forgiveness, whether for themselves or for others for their healing within. I am here to face my own demons with my own tendency to be selfish, for example. I am here in part to be less self-indulgent and to help me think more about others first, rather than about myself, which is my own weakness."

Mahesh, who was also sat on the floor, was quietly listening to the friend's conversations. He smiled and nodded as if to acknowledge Puvan's comments, though each had been strangers until their recent meeting at the ashram.

Mahesh's skin was as dark as chocolate he was slight in stature and stood only about five feet and six inches tall. He was usually dressed all in white, as were the rest of the friends most of the time and for any visits to the ashram this was a prerequisite and being white clothing it was to show an intention of trying to purify one's own soul of all that was negative, as best as possible for each individual concerned. Mahesh, either found it hard to reveal his own reasons for visiting Swami or he just wanted to keep such reasons private and therefore to himself.

Mahesh, simply added to the friend's conversation by adding, "We are all lucky to be here. Swami, has called us here in our souls to visit now. The reason will perhaps be unknown to us for all our lives. Maybe, only in some future life-time, for each of us will the reason for our being here now, be revealed to us!"

"Wise words, perhaps," replied Joshua.

The friends fell silent for a while and looked at each other and smiled. Mahesh, held his hands together as a gesture and said to the rest of the group, "namaste," meaning, 'the God within me, see's the God in you'!

That night Joshua had a dream. In the dream, Papa Luca came to him dressed just like Swami in an orange robe and he held out the same ring that Swami had manifested for Joshua, a few days earlier. Papa Luca did not speak, but simply smiled and placed it on the finger of Joshua's right hand. As he did so Joshua felt himself transform into the four-year-old boy that he had once been, many years earlier in his life. Joshua, had grown up in a family with one younger sister and with both of his parents, his father was kind to him but stern too, in part owing to his own experiences during the second world war. His mother had been a young bride to his own father and Joshua in turn was born when his mother was in her early twenties. She had returned to work soon after he was born and so Joshua in his formative years was raised for much of the time by his maternal grandmother. She was a kind woman but in her early sixties by this time and worn out by her own life's sadness and experiences.

Joshua, realised in his dream that he had not as a very young child for some reason felt secure sub-consciously and which had in turn led to him feeling insecure and anxious, both as a child and as a teenager and later in adulthood. He had experienced a lack of self-confidence for most of his life to date. In his dream, he felt Papa Luca, on giving him the gift of the ring – that Swami had manifested for him, that it was representative of these perceived difficulties in his own upbringing. He also knew in his dream that they were in fact his own life's challenges which were part of his own karma he had to face and overcome through his own feelings of self-love and self-nurture.

Joshua, awoke clearly remembering the dream. He looked at the ring still on his right hand that Swami had recently given to him. He smiled and felt an inner knowing with greater depth as to the reason why Swami had given him the ring. It was a reminder to him to face life's challenges and to focus on his own loving connection to the universal love that surrounds all of humanity and creation, and is within all, whenever he felt unloved or unappreciated, to help him cope and get through such times. Joshua, said a prayer of thanks to both Papa-Luca and Swami with his own deeper sense of self-realisation of these facts.

Joshua, thought to himself in that moment that he was blessed. He asked that humanity be blessed and healed of its suffering. That humanity, might soon wake up to this divine connection to the divine spirit within all!

***

The next morning Joshua got dressed as his friends were also starting to stir, it was still early and dark outside. They all planned to walk together to the ashram in the hope of getting an early queue-line to get close to Swami once they were inside if they could manage to do so. They always desired a sitting space inside the small hall, near the seat of the 'Cosmic Avatar' – Swami-Baba.

Puvan, woke from his sleep and dragged himself out of bed as he was always a bit surly in the mornings. John likewise but was often quieter, Mahesh as always, introverted but smiling.

"Did you sleep well?" Mahesh asked Joshua.

"Yes, good thanks. I had an interesting dream which featured the ring which Swami gave to me. The message was partially about learning to love myself more and not to be always seeking it from others, especially women!"

"Yes, yes, very good. I understand," replied Mahesh shaking his head sideways as he spoke and he continued,

"When Swami comes to you in a dream it is very auspicious, so you are very blessed."

"I remember my dreams often now. But I have only had a few featuring Swami," replied Joshua.

Each of the four friends grabbed some bread and jam that they had saved and walked outside into the fresh still night air, it was still only four a.m. but dedicated as they were to their own spiritual practice, they wanted their best chance to sit at the feet of Swami-Baba.

***

The four friends got their seats luckily back at the feet of the master-teacher. Swami, walked into the large room this time in a white robe, but barefoot as usual. Standing just over five feet tall and of slight build he was not much bigger in stature than a child. His face was often serious for the most part, his right-hand palm, facing upwards and often moving in a circular motion at waist height for some mysterious reason as if blessing the room and those in it, it is said, to raise the energy and consciousness of those present and perhaps beyond.

Joshua, sat transfixed with his legs crossed and dressed all in white like his three friends. Swami-Baba's halo was still clearly visible around his head, at least to Joshua, which he never mentioned that he could see, to his friends for whatever reason. At the time Joshua, still could not fully appreciate his good fortune just to be in the presence of this great teacher who's return to Earth had long been prophesised.

A member of the audience, a middle aged western woman, with short greying hair and wearing a pair of pearl-earrings and which automatically made her look rather middle-class, handed a photo to Swami and asked, "Swami, is this a correct impression of Jesus Christ the Messiah, in the photo?" The photo being like an x-ray photo of an impression of what looked like a picture of the shadow of the profile of Jesus.

Swami, took the photo as the woman asked again, "Swami, is this what Jesus looked like?"

Swami, held the photo in his left palm and he ran his other palm facing downwards over the photo and then he held up the photograph to the audience.

"Photo, now blank," he said in English, to the audience. Swami, could speak a little English without always having the need of the interpreter stood beside him as usual.

Swami, then ran his hand back in the opposite direction with the photo lying flat on his other palm.

He held the photo up for all to see - a photographic picture of Jesus had magically appeared on the photographic paper in place of the earlier picture. The audience gasped and applauded.

"This is what he looked like!" said Swami, holding the photo aloft for all to see.

Joshua, remembered at that moment, reading about a time that a visiting devotee was given by Swami, a small wooden cross on a chain and being told by Swami that the wood that small cross was made of was from the actual cross on which Jesus was crucified!

Swami, proceeded to give a talk about unconditional love and listening and always following the conscience. The audience listened with a great reverence for Swami's words. After a few bhajans by some of the Indian audience present in the hall, Swami exited the hall.

On their way, back to their accommodation on the edge of town, the four friends chatted about the manifestation of the photo of Jesus. Joshua, said to the group of men, "It has always been my wish to have met Jesus. Today, I saw a photo of who I do believe to be the real Jesus, manifested by someone just as special as Jesus himself. How lucky were we?"

The other men nodded in agreement and smiled at their joint good fortune, blessed to be present at what had occurred before their eyes, as if by magic!"

***

It was the last morning in Kodaikanal for the group of friends. They had all planned to take a twelve-hour bus ride from the old hill station town to Bangalore to save money. There they all planned to visit Swami for a few more days at another of Swami's ashrams, in a small town called Whitefield, near the city of Bangalore and had decided to travel together on the same bus. Just before Joshua got on the bus with his green canvas backpack, he purchased some food from a small café at the bus-station. Soon after he had eaten it the bus set off on the journey firstly for a three-hour ride down a bumpy dirt road to the bottom of the mountain. Joshua, started to feel unwell soon after setting off and was starting to have to repeatedly vomit out of the window of the bus. His friend John, who was also feeling unwell himself with a virus, kindly pulling him back from the bus window before any oncoming buses passed by and travelling in the opposite direction on the road, this being to prevent Joshua from being hurt by any passing vehicle. This went on for hours, Joshua becoming increasingly delirious from his suspected food-poisoning and John getting more and more exhausted from having to yank his head out of the window into the safe confines of the bus itself. At one stage the bus during the night filled with a swarm of hundreds of thousands of locusts which had entered through the windows of the bus open because of the hot temperature on the flat plains and the bus being too old to have air-conditioning. In the end, so, delirious did Joshua become that he later forgot all about the locust invasion until being reminded of it by his friend John many years later after the event.

Finally, the next morning the bus reached its destination much to Joshua's relief. He just needed to lie down somewhere for a couple of days to recover from his sickness, he felt. Swami, it transpired would not arrive at the ashram, until after the group of friends had flown back home to their native countries.

Joshua, was too sick to care about that and was instead grateful for the time at his disposal to recover more fully before his return home and spent most of his time there sleeping after the traumatic bus journey.

John's flight back to England was a couple of days after Joshua's, so, they hugged and bid each other farewell and promised to keep in touch with each other in the future.

***

Joshua, arrived back home in England a few days later. His last days being spent recuperating from the serious case of food-poisoning that he had unfortunately had to face for both his long journey across much of India on a bus with his friends and then while still resting at his final Indian destination at the ashram near the city of Bangalore but without seeing Swami again after he left Kodaikanal.

He was only just beginning to digest his life changing experience in India, when he was back sat at his favourite café in his sea-side home town and was thinking as he drank a cup of tea with pleasure, how in India, or anywhere else for that matter he could never find a cup of tea to match those he drank when at home.

As Joshua sat by the window of the Galley Café, he stared out of the window. A familiar figure passed in front of him, an elderly man smiled through the window at Joshua as he did so – it was Papa Luca, his elderly and wise mysterious friend.

Papa Luca came into the café and stood opposite Joshua and asked him, "Do you mind if I join you Joshua. I hear you have just returned from a very interesting adventure in Southern India. Am I not correct?"

"Yes, correct. How did you know that I have just been out there?" replied Joshua.

"Ah, I know many things! I hear you went to visit the famous Indian Avatar, Swami-Baba, correct?" replied Papa Luca.

"Correct. How come you know of him Papa Luca?" replied Joshua.

"As I just said Joshua, I know about many things. I thought you knew that my friend?" said Papa Luca.

He smiled and winked at Joshua as he spoke.

"Yes, I know you do. But for some reason I did not expect you to know about Swami-Baba, as he lives so far from here. What is it that you know about him then?" said Joshua.

"I know that he is a Cosmic Avatar – whereas Jesus, it is said, was a Planetary Avatar in comparison. Which makes you my friend, more than fortunate. More than enviable, by many. That was a once in a lifetime's opportunity was it not, my young friend? You must tell me all about," said Papa Luca, as he ordered himself a coffee from the waitress and made himself comfortable to be regaled by Joshua, with some of his stories about his recent adventure to India.

"What did you make of Swami, yourself then?" Papa Luca asked Joshua.

"From the first time that I saw Swami and each time thereafter, I noticed that there was a sort of 'halo' around and above his head, like a sort of haze. I could not believe what I was seeing at first. As I looked and doubted my own eyes, the halo around his head suddenly grew until it filled the hall-room that we were all sat in at the time. Then suddenly I saw it shot back, to just being about a foot wide around his head. It was as if Swami could hear my own thoughts and doubts about what my own eyes were seeing at that time!" replied Joshua.

"Yes, yes. Go on," said Papa Luca. Joshua, continued to speak, "There was another time after he gave a talk at Easter-time that an impression of a picture even appeared of Jesus Christ's face in the velvet upholstery material of the chair that Swami had been sat in during the darshan that morning. It was amazing. Again, it was easy to doubt your own eyes! My own doubts kept on pervading my own thoughts."

"Yes, yes. But that is your pattern, Joshua. It has been your pattern for so long now. You are constantly battling with your own thoughts, are you not? True?" said Papa Luca.

"True, true. I know, it is so annoying and a constant struggle. I am still learning to trust. To simply trust. In so many things which I doubt. God especially. And my own connection to God," replied Joshua.

"Yes, yes. To the very God of which you and I – and all of creation – is! And is a part of both. Simultaneously," replied Papa Luca.

"Yes, I know. But, I have returned home, a different person to the one who left, somehow! I know that I have only just arrived back home, but I can feel the difference in myself. It is as if a part of Swami-Baba has returned with me, in some strange sort of mystical way," said Joshua.

"Either that, or you have left behind in India part of you. A part of you that you no longer required," said Papa Luca.

"Yes, it does feel a bit like that. It is as if I have left behind some of my old pain. Some of my old pain habit behind. I feel, spiritually reinvigorated, somehow. I met some interesting people there, everyone, that I saw had a clarity in their eyes and an inner beauty, stillness and radiance, it seemed to shine out from their being somehow. One person I met, was called John he lives near here and I hope to keep in close touch with him."

"Good," said Papa Luca. He continued and said, "Your time in India was predestined. It was meant to be. From the highest realms, you were invited to go! It could only be so, for it to happen. For to meet the Cosmic-

Avatar of the age, is far beyond being fortunate or lucky, you know?" You were indeed blessed to be there, at what was the right time for you. It will stay with you always, it was a blessing, as it was and is for all who visit Swami-Baba. Know, and trust that, if nothing else. May you through that experience recall in time who you also are, who we all are and may you come to know, come to trust and come to share that knowledge with many others. The purpose of that, being to help raise the consciousness of humanity around the globe. That may now sound like a wild fantasy or a dream. But, such things will come to pass Joshua. In the not too distant future my young friend." With that Papa Luca finished his drink, stood up from his seat and quietly left the café and disappeared into the now bustling crowd. Joshua, observed him through the somewhat misty glass window of the café as he did so. Joshua, immersed himself thinking about the conversation which had just taken place and how strange a man, Papa Luca seemed to be."

***

Joshua, longed for romance in his life. He longed to hold some special woman in his arms with whom he could find a deep love with. It was his dream and greatest desire, to find such. It had been such for all his adult life. In fact, from the age of fourteen, when he fell in love – which turned out to be infatuation – be it a then testing – one sided infatuation and which annoyingly in hindsight lasted and preoccupied him throughout his later school years.

In that regard perhaps, Joshua, was more like a woman, with his dreams of romance, but at the same time he was masculine and courageous in his being and in his heart and mind he had always been drawn to physical outdoor pursuits and sports. Joshua, was not much of a team player, which was a skill he would only learn much later in life through his own often induced hardship and distress.

Joshua, stood six feet tall and was quite athletic in his build, his hair was short and dark and because he did enjoy female company and after the heart-break of one long-term relationship, he was determined to find love again. This time however, he was looking for something different, first and foremost – that was inner beauty in the other person. He had learnt the importance of such. To not find it in a person could be to one's own great cost in one's own life and until the lesson was learnt, that physical beauty could sometimes be only skin deep.

Joshua, decided it was time for another visit to one of his favourite 'spiritual' places – 'Glastonbury', a small town in the old 'Isle of Avalon' and a place steeped in myth and legend. Joshua, loved the town since his early twenties when his own spiritual journey seeking his own answers to life had begun in earnest.

Joshua, jumped into his old silver car which he loved and set off alone for the day but determined to meet up with his old and dear friend Peter, who had become over recent years a mentor and something of a father figure to him.

Peter, was a gardener and about sixty years of age, he had a roving eye and lived in a caravan, he was in truth just an old 'hippy' at heart and with a deep sensitivity to spirit. Joshua, had seen Peter as a friend and teacher because of his spiritual aptitude, he thought to himself, as he sped along the country lanes between his sea-side home and the sacred place to which he headed – Glastonbury.

On arrival, Joshua, decided because of his recent trip to see Swami-Baba in India that he should visit the Swami-Baba centre in the town, this being the place which had first inspired his idea to visit Swami and to germinate when he was given a book by an elderly lady by chance on a previous visit.

Peter, worked at a large house next door to the spiritual centre, which was owned by a retired airline pilot and his wife. They had visited the Indian avatar many years earlier with life-changing results.

Joshua found Peter in the greenhouse tending to his plants as usual and so he crept up on Peter to surprise him. Without turning Peter said, "Hello, Joshua, I sensed your visit today. How are you my friend? It has been a while since your last visit, hasn't it?"

"I know it has Peter. I do apologise. But I have been rather busy. I have only just returned from a three week visit to see Swami-Baba in India," said Joshua.

"Oh, how exciting! We must go inside to the centre next door then and share a pot of tea, then you can tell me all about your trip. I am ready for a cup myself. I have been in the greenhouse already for hours this morning it feels," replied Peter. With that both friends hugged and smiled at each other. Like father and son, it always felt. At least to Joshua it did. To him it always felt like a special relationship and he was sure it felt the same for Peter, too! They entered the old stables building, converted many years before into a small bed and breakfast establishment which doubled up when required, to be a spiritual centre for people either interested in, or who were already devotees of Swami-Baba. Joshua, was still filled with enthusiasm about his recent trip which he wished to share with his dear friend, Peter.

"Hello, Pam. Hello Samantha!" said Joshua, speaking to the two elderly women and who looked after the premises, for the retired pilot.

"How are you Joshua? Lovely to see you again," replied Samantha.

"How was your visit to Swami-Baba, Joshua? We can't wait to hear all about it!" replied Pam.

"It was quite an adventure. Can Peter and I have a cup of tea first. We are both looking forward to a cup," said Joshua.

"Of course, you can dear. I will put on the kettle now. Sit yourselves down," said Pam with her usual friendly demeanour.

"Oh, by the way Joshua, my daughter Tina is coming along to visit shortly, have you met her before, Joshua?" said Samantha.

"No, I don't think so," replied Joshua.

"I think you might like her," said Samantha with a smile.

"I will look forward to meeting her, I like meeting new people. What is she like?" replied Joshua.

"Lovely, of course, she is my daughter, after all," replied Samantha.

"Of course, she is," replied Joshua diplomatically.

"If she is half as lovely as you, she will be beautiful. I am sure," continued Joshua.

"Oh, stop it," replied Samantha blushing.

Peter and Joshua sat down to drink their tea. It soon transpired that a meditation afternoon had been arranged at the centre for about the same time Peter and Joshua had arrived. They decided to stay and join those who also arrived for the meeting at the centre.

An attractive woman aged about thirty-five years of age and with long dark straight hair sat down next to Joshua and introduced herself to him, "Hello, my name is Tina," the woman said.

"I am Joshua, nice to meet you," he replied.

The meditation commenced with about twenty different people attending the meeting in total. Joshua, being experienced at meditation, felt comfortable and at ease with the practice as it was so familiar to him. Within no time of the meditation session beginning, Joshua, became aware of a very strong and intense sensation of love coming from his heart and chest area and going straight to the woman named Tina who was sat right next to him. Joshua, tried to stay calm and as detached as possible from the emotion of love that he felt pouring from him to her. He knew that he had never met this woman before in his life but the incredibly powerful waves of love continued to flow to her from him and throughout the duration of the meditation in which all the people present were taking part and lasted for about fifteen minutes. The intensity of the love he felt was so intense, so strong, that Joshua immediately knew that it would almost be painful to step out of it. In fact, to no longer be in this woman's presence would be painful, he thought to himself.

At the end of the meditation, Joshua turned and smiled at the dark-haired woman sat next to him. She smiled back and said simply, "that was nice!"

"What was?" replied Joshua.

"The meditation," she said still smiling.

"Yes, yes. It was," replied Joshua. He did not, at that time, wish to divulge the intense feeling of love he had moments earlier felt for the woman sat next to him. 'I wonder if she felt it to', Joshua simply thought to himself. A little while later after everyone had a chance to get up and mingle amongst the other people present at the meeting, Joshua grabbed his friend Peter by the arm and said to him, "Peter, see that dark-haired woman over there, who I was sat next to during the meditation – well I felt something throughout it, that I have never felt in such a way. As soon as the meditation started I just felt waves of this incredibly strong feeling of love go from my heart to her. The whole time. Yes, the whole time. There must be a strong connection between us. I don't know what it is. But, I know I can find out. I will try to see later if we can sit together somewhere quiet and I can ask my guides what it is all about."

"Good idea, I would. It sounds like something very special to me. How lucky are you?" said Peter.

"Yes, I suppose so," said Joshua, slightly negatively.

Peter looked at Joshua and seeing his concern, simply said, "Joshua, don't be afraid of love. It might be the only time in your life you ever find it! You never know. At least explore it. Ask the questions if you wish from where it comes and what connection you have with her. But do make sure you explore it first. Before you walk away that is, for I know you, remember!" said Peter smiling, as he placed a hand on both of Joshua's shoulders as he looked him straight in the eyes as he spoke, "Love is very precious. Some people spend lifetimes looking for such a love and never manage to find it. If you walk away out of fear of being hurt, or even if she is not your type for whatever reason, you may live to regret it, Joshua. Explore it, spend time with her. Nothing happens by coincidence. We have known each other for a long time now. I know that you, like me, have been looking for a love like this for a long time. It is your dream, as it is my dream and as it is also the dream of every other person who walks this Earth. Find out more. Please find out more and give love a chance, please!"

Joshua, after his conversation with Peter about the rarity of souls who find true love in life, decided he should at least try to find out more about the reason for the connection with Tina, where at least for him magic seemed to occur. Joshua, went over to speak with her as she was sat with friends seemingly deep in in thought. Joshua, wondered if she was thinking about happened between them both earlier not knowing what she felt at the time of the meditation.

"Hi, how are you doing?" said Joshua to the dark-haired woman.

"Yes, good thanks. By the way I am Samantha's daughter, who helps here. I believe you know her?"

"Oh, yes, I do. So, how come you are here today, Tina?" replied Joshua.

"I am here to visit my sister who lives not far from here. My mother invited me to visit the centre here. She has been telling me stories about Swami-Baba and I became interested because of the things that she had told me about him. I hear that you have only just returned from India after visiting him. How was your trip?

What might I ask, did you yourself make of him? Was he someone like Jesus, as many say he is?" she enquired.

"Yes, I believe he is. He is not an ordinary mortal in any sense, in my opinion. I feel privileged to have had the opportunity to go and visit him. They say that you are called on some level and it only occurs if it is meant to happen, meeting him I mean!" replied Joshua.

"Oh, I see. I didn't know that," replied Tina.

Joshua, changed the subject and said to her, "Tina, we seem to have a strong connection and to me it was obvious from something I felt in my meditation. I would like to find out more about it. I have developed an ability through many years of meditation, a bit like a medium I suppose. I can ask questions of spirit and I hear the answers to my questions in my mind which I believe come to me from somewhere in my soul or the ocean of consciousness even, as I like to call it! Do you mind spending a bit of time together, so that I could do that to find out more about our special connection?"

"Yes, I would like to find out more about it too. I felt it as well. I could feel a tremendous amount of love between us. Despite the fact, I have never met you and know nothing about you. Yes, I think we should find out more about it, if you can do that? Where do you propose and when? I am going back with Davina my sister, to her house shortly, which is very close by. Would you like to come back to too, perhaps we could try and find out more there?" Tina replied.

"Yes, that would be great!" replied Joshua.

Tina, travelled with her sister Davina to the house and Peter drove Joshua there soon after, as he already knew the way, having visited there on a previous occasion.

Joshua, soon found himself in a room which Tina's sister used for her healing work, and so it already had a peaceful and tranquil energy. Joshua, sat on the floor with his legs crossed and Tina sat opposite him. Joshua, went into his meditation and began to ask spirit in his mind the reason for their deep connection which had triggered the deep sense of love that Joshua had felt arise from his heart which had then passed straight to Tina as she was sat next to him earlier at the Swami-Baba Centre.

Joshua, was told by his spirit guides, "My son, you were both together in a previous life-time when you were both of the same tribe on the plains of North America several hundred years ago. You were both deeply in love with each other. However, during that time, you my son, were struck down with an illness resulting in a heavy fever and you died. You were both young at the time. She never got over her loss in that life-time. Your soul's each made a promise, while both of you were in the spirit realm to meet again in this life-time. It is of course the choice for each of you whether you both choose to pursue your love further in this life-time, for you are different people in this life-time and with different traits and issues even though, it is your soul's which are intrinsically the same and are of course eternal. It was due to and from the memory held deep in both of your own soul's where such memories are stored that the out-pouring of love that you felt for each other sprung."

Having received the information, Joshua came out of his meditation having thanked his spirit guides for their help to relay this information to him. He told Tina what he was told by spirit. Tina replied,

"During your meditation, I was not spoken to. However, instead I was shown a series of pictures which fitted exactly, the story that you have just told me. I believe what you have told me is true because of what I too was shown. Thank you, Joshua."

They both hugged each other for some time, knowing how special that their connection was and how rare it was to discover something so special.

However, in his heart Joshua, already knew that he would probably not pursue things further. His pain from his previous marriage break up and his new resulting fear of commitment stood sadly between them both, despite even all that he had learnt up to this point in his life. The most difficult thing for him would be never knowing how a relationship between them both would have turned out! Would it have been blessed or would it not? That is the price we sometimes must pay for our choices in life, as Joshua would come to learn!

***

'Christmas seemed to come earlier this year', Joshua, thought to himself as he sat in his favourite window seat in the Galley Café, back in his home town. A few weeks had passed since he had met Tina at the Swami-Baba Centre in Glastonbury. He had decided after much deliberation, not to pursue any sort of relationship with her that is even assuming if she had wanted to do so, and of course she might not have either, despite the deep soul love that he had felt for her, which might seem strange, unusual or downright stupid to so many other people, especially bearing in mind the special rarity of such a meeting, or a divine present of sorts. He did not know Tina's feelings or whether she herself would have wanted to get involved in any relationship with him. He never asked, instead he just assumed that she would have. Assumption, was perhaps one of Joshua's weakness's, 'he was only human after all,' he thought to himself.

Joshua, had done much soul searching about the matter when to his relief, he happened to see his old friend Papa Luca walk into the Galley Café and order a drink.

"May I join you, Joshua?" said Papa Luca with his usual twinkle in his eyes.

"Of course, you can, it would be a pleasure," replied Joshua.

Papa Luca took a seat opposite Joshua, and said, "I heard you had a rather rare meeting with a young woman recently which turned out to be rather special, Joshua?"

"Yes, that's right. How did you know that?" asked Joshua, rather surprised that Papa Luca seemed to know, yet again, mysteriously all about some intimate part of his own life – which he had not shared with anyone other than his friend Peter.

"Joshua, you and I are also connected on a very deep level which I might share with you one day. But, only when the time is right, if I feel it to be so. I am happy to discuss further, the meeting you had with the young woman in question and the significance of that meeting to you in your own life. That is if you wish to speak about it Joshua?"

"Of course, yes, we may speak about it. I feel that I have looked in depth at the matter. I seem to have come to terms not to pursue any relationship with her. I all along assumed she would have, if I had chosen to," said Joshua.

"You were right in that assumption, on this occasion! You could have chosen to enter a relationship with her. There was karma between you both. It would have been a good opportunity. However, it would have meant you having to make many sacrifices, for it to be a happy union of souls. You both desired different things in many cases. There would have been much love and harmony, not to mention probably children, that is if you had chosen that path! But, you have other ambitions do you not Joshua? And you were not prepared to make those sacrifices, were you?"

"Yes, you are right," replied Joshua with a sadness in his voice as he spoke.

He continued, "I cannot really explain it – part of me wants more than anything to be loved, adored and taken care of. Even mothered to some extent. However, I know that would annoy me no end and eventually drive me crazy and causing no end of damage to such a relationship. I know now that I need to find the love that

I am seeking from others from inside my own self, instead of from outside my own self. I need to keep on remembering that 'I am love'. That I am loved, that I am the source of that love and that we are all a part of God in truth," said Joshua.

"Yes, yes, correct! You are that. We are all that. That is the purpose of life here in the physical realm. We are here to remember our spiritual essence that we all share. The real us. That we are all, each one of us divine love. We are all spiritual beings having a physical experience through being here on Earth in a physical body. You are right, Joshua.

Either choice would have been correct, there was no wrong choice. You have made your choice. The only price you will pay is never knowing in full how your choice might have turned out in comparison to any similar choice, should you choose in the future," replied Papa Luca.

"Yes, I agree, that was the conclusion I came to within my own self," said Joshua.

Papa Luca replied, "Yes, know you must move on now. Do not look back. Respect and accept the choices you made and move forward with confidence and acceptance until the next moment that the divine taps you on the shoulder with such a magical offering. You are blessed Joshua. Your desire is to grow and to be always good and kind. I respect you for that."

With that Papa Luca stood up smiling and made his excuses and left the café, as he did so he looked over his shoulder once at Joshua and gave him a wave and disappeared into the busy crowd of Christmas shoppers outside.

***

Joshua, was stood looking at his own reflection in the mirror in his bedroom, he was now in his mid-thirties in age, he was slim and athletic in appearance. He had always looked after himself and prided himself on his own appearance. His dark hair was short and straight usually he was clean shaven, he had experienced severe acne as a teenager which had left him with a rugged appearance which he had grown into, he had blue eyes and knew that they were indeed the window into the soul of most individual's, he knew that he was also an old soul!

Joshua, had always tried hard to be a good and considerate person and that was his greatest ambition, besides finding true love. The only thing which motivated him more each day was to find the answers: the answers to the mysteries of life!

***

'My soul is immortal', Joshua thought to himself. He had been suffering a bit with health anxiety to which he was prone. It drove him crazy, which he thought was rather ironic! Like many people, Joshua's main battle in life had always been with himself, or perhaps rather with his own mind. When he was, a teenager he had enjoyed the process of exploring his own thoughts, which was why he spent so much time thinking. His father would say to Joshua, "Joshua, you live in a dream world!" and it was true, Joshua realised that he did, but only after he was much older. What was once a pleasure turned into a living hell, for one day his mind seemed to turn against him and so a new chapter in his life began.

What had once been a pleasant time exploring his own thoughts, which he found intriguing and interesting had become a fearful and anxiety inducing experience. As a child, he had been prone to worry and as he had grown older his mental battles he believed were just a part of perhaps some form of character weakness, or maybe, just a rite of passage, until his own real true character would emerge, stronger and wiser, on the other side of an anxious period in his life and from which he did eventually emerge to his great relief. His own spiritual journey was primarily an inner journey that had helped him through his inner turmoil. Joshua, was always grateful that he managed this process without medication and that he instead learned to live with and deal with his own fears and emotions in a more holistic and alternative way. Ultimately his own deep belief in his own spiritual connection to 'all that is,' pulled him through his dark time and this taught him to always appreciate beauty. However, he had learnt during his own life that physical beauty was only skin deep, that the essence of physical beauty itself in the human form was also a hostage to the passage of time, eventually turning to dust blown in the wind. However, inner beauty on the other hand had its own immortality and delivered its own treasure to the holder, with that in mind he would focus his love interest on that which he could see and feel in those that he met to whom he felt being drawn in terms of a relationship concerning matters of love. Joshua, was always a romantic at heart!

***

Joshua, was sat on the veranda of the Harbour Inn, one of his favourite places to spend time when down by the beach.

The place was run and owned by a man called Stanley who was in his eighties in age and still had a lot of hair for someone his age which he tied back. He had ten children and it was said that he had once been a monk and that he had lived in the Himalaya Mountains in Tibet, a mystical land which had a strong pull for Joshua to visit, a land he had never had the opportunity to set foot upon.

Joshua strangely had also, recently begun to have vivid dreams of visiting a monastery high up in the snow laden slopes on a mountain somewhere in Tibet. In his dream, Joshua would find himself as an old man and being visited by his current 'younger self'. He would sit at the feet of his older-self and meditate with the other monks and when he had a question, to which he sought an answer, he would sit and speak to and ask questions of the older version of himself. The questions were always about ways that his younger self could best deal with and ultimately vanquish the fears in the younger version of himself.

"Hello, Joshua, how are you?" asked Stanley pleased to see him.

"Good, thank you Stanley, how are you?"

"Very well, Joshua," he replied with a smile.

Joshua continued, "I have started to have these strange dreams about visiting a Monastery in Tibet and being greeted there by an older version of myself."

"Then it sounds to me that you are being called to visit Tibet, Joshua. You might have heard that I once lived there for several years when in my twenties, as a monk. I thought that I would be there all my life. It was not to be, because I felt the pull to come and live in England by the sea and here I still am fifty years later, still married and having had ten children, now I also have sixteen grand-children. I only run this bar and restaurant to escape!" Stanley laughed out loud with a chuckle. Although, he was in his eighties, Stanley had more of the energy of and presence of a sixty-year-old hippy!

"Stanley, what drew you to visit Tibet and then become a monk for several years?" asked Joshua.

Stanley replied, "I just knew it was something I had to do then. It was my destiny I suppose. I think I knew deep down it was a short-term thing. It was just a journey I had to go on back then. But, really it was a journey into myself. A journey to find my own real self," Stanley replied.

"And did you? Did you find yourself through that experience?" asked Joshua.

"Yes, I did Joshua," replied Stanley.

"I think that might also be where I need to go next. Perhaps to find the next bit of myself that I am seeking," said Joshua.

"If you must. You must. I still have a contact at the Monastery I stayed at. It is the son of my teacher who is now a monk and a teacher there. Here is his name and where you can find him," replied Stanley.

Stanley with that gave to Joshua a tatty old address card in gold lettering which read –

'Rinpoche Sun Yin

The Potala Palace,

Lhasa,

TIBET.

Joshua, took the card from Stanley and stared at it for a few seconds. Joshua, knew intuitively this was the next place that he had to travel to and to continue his own spiritual journey and to discover the answers to the questions that he still had inside of himself about his own life!

***

The taxi was driven into Lhasa at night. The full moon was a bright orb of light cresting the Himalaya mountain backdrop and ahead in the distance high on an escarpment Joshua caught his first glimpse of the Potala Palace the winter home of the Dalai-Lama since the seventh century which the current Dalia Lama had not visited since China's rule over Tibet in 1959 after he fled to live in neighbouring India.

As the taxi approached the Palace, Joshua could hear the stones on the dirt road crunching under the taxi's tyres, as the ground had already started to freeze in the icy cold night air. The night sky was radiant with stars and the outline of the massive Palace was clear to see because of the light from the full moon.

The taxi pulled up in front of the large wooden gates at the Palace entrance. A monk opened the gates from inside of the courtyard and the taxi drove into the large Palace courtyard. Joshua, noticed prayer wheels all around the outer edges of the courtyard covered in shiny old cobble stones. The taxi was greeted by the same monk who had just earlier opened the heavy main gates. The monk opened the rear door of the taxi where Joshua was sitting.

The monk was wearing a deep purple cloak with a heavy cream woollen fleece over the outside and a thick brown sheep-skin hat. His big round Tibetan features gave out a big smile, as he said, "Hello, you must be Joshua. Stanley rang me to say you would be arriving late, as you have. How was your journey? Oh, I am Rinpoche Sun Yin. I believe Stanley mentioned me to you, a few weeks ago. It is a pleasure to meet you my friend. Let me take your baggage."

Sun Yin, spoke excellent English, but with an American accent having spent several years studying theology at Harvard many years previous.

"Thank you, I am very tired after my long journey. This is just like my dream. I believe I was meant to come here now for some reason," replied Joshua.

"Yes, you are right. It is your destiny to come and visit Tibet and this Palace or you would not have come. Welcome, welcome, Joshua my friend," said Sun-Yin smiling.

"Come, come, follow me into the Palace before you get too cold my friend." continued Sun Yin and as he helped Joshua with his bags they both entered the main entrance of the ancient building which was filled with an atmosphere and feeling which Joshua had never experienced in his lifetime before but was at the same time strangely familiar. The energy inside was like that of a medieval Cathedral in England, but this was Tibet and the Palace exuded what it was: a Tibetan Palace, high in the highest mountains on Earth – The Himalaya.

***

Sun Yin said to Joshua, "How was your trip and how is my good friend, Stanley? I have not seen him for many years. He was a wonderful monk you know when he lived here."

"My trip here was long and very tiring Sun Yin, and I did not know until recently that he had been a Buddhist monk once," replied Joshua.

"Stanley, was here many years ago, when I was very young. He stood out then because he was the only western monk that we have ever had here at the Potala Palace Monastery, as usually Tibetan monks are not surprisingly, usually from Tibet," said Sun Yin laughing.

"Of course," replied Joshua smiling.

Joshua, took some time to take in his new surroundings. The Palace was full of lit candles and there were many old looking Tibetan tapestries adorning the walls and many statues, some made of wood and beautifully carved and representative of the Buddha himself, many were painted in gold.

Sun Yin, was sat on a big cushion in the large ornate room with his legs crossed and said, "Why did you feel it was necessary for you to visit Tibet now, Joshua. It is a long way from home?"

"After Stanley mentioned to me only recently, about his connection to this Palace, I knew that I had to come. He told me about you, Sun Yin. I felt it was no coincidence and felt drawn to visit. I have long been drawn to Tibet and its spiritual influences on things," replied Joshua.

"Indeed, I feel it too, you were meant to come here now for some reason. All will unfold soon as to the reason why," said Sun Yin.

"Yes, I am sure too," said Joshua.

"I will take you to your room so you can sleep Joshua, you are very tired of course, I can see. We will talk more tomorrow," said Sun Yin.

***

Early the next morning, Joshua was woken up by some chanting noise coming from outside the Palace as the windows were only covered with wooden shutters.

He could also hear the prayer wheels turning in the Palace courtyard. It was a ritual for all the monks at the Palace monastery to walk twelve times around the perimeter of the courtyard turning the prayer wheels as they passed them offering prayers to the Buddha himself.

Joshua, wiped the sleepy dust from his eyes after he had been given a large old four-poster bed to sleep in and covered in many beautiful thick Tibetan embroidered blankets to keep him warm from the cold night air outside the Palace.

Joshua, opened the wooden shutters and was greeted by a clear cloudless deep blue sky, a magnificent view of the Himalaya mountains circled the Palace for three-hundred and sixty degrees as Lhasa and the Palace above the city sat in a valley surrounded by the snow-covered peaks, the city itself sitting thousands of metres above sea-level.

A Palace servant led Joshua down to a large dining-room. Sun Yin dressed as always in his monk's Tibetan attire greeted him with his palms held together at chest height and Joshua returned the greeting of 'namaste'.

"I hear you were recently in India visiting the great Swami-Baba, is that not so, Joshua?" enquired Sun Yin.

"Yes, that's right," replied Joshua.

"I have heard many stories about the great Swami-Baba. What did you make of him, Joshua?" said Sun Yin.

"He was very special, not a normal human being at all. Every time that I saw him he had a hazy sort of halo around his head. I saw him manifest various objects too, from thin air!" replied Joshua.

Joshua, held out his right hand and showed Sun Yin the gold ring on his finger with the green emerald surrounded by the two cobra heads encrusted in diamonds that Swami-Baba manifested and gave to him.

"Can I see the ring please, Joshua," said Sun Yin.

Joshua removed the ring from his finger and handed it to Sun Yin.

Sun Yin, held the ring in both hands for a while with his eyes shut as he did so.

"I feel much love from this ring. It was given to you by someone capable of great love. It was a gift and reminder for you to remember who you are. A part of the loving force which surrounds and contains all of us. It is a special gift Joshua," said Sun Yin.

"Yes, it is, I wear it every day and it means a lot to me, especially as Swami-Baba manifested it with his own hands and then gave it to me himself on my recent trip there. I had many magical experiences there and which I will always remember, I am sure. At that time, I feel that I made the transition in to manhood, it is hard to explain!" replied Joshua.

Sun Yin, did not reply he just smiled knowingly at Joshua. A look that Joshua would become accustomed to.

***

"This afternoon in the monastery, all of the monks here will attend as they do each day, meditation for an hour in the great hall of divinity. The Palace monks with the Dalai-Lama, until his exile to India, would all meditate together in this sacred place. Please come and join us later," said Sun Yin to Joshua.

With that Sun Yin handed Joshua a monk's robe and left for him to change into it for the occasion.

"Thank you so much. I would love to join you all," replied Joshua.

"Two o' clock this afternoon – I will see you in the monastery-room then Joshua. I will leave you until then to look around and to feel free," said Sun Yin.

Following the invitation, Joshua found himself sat in the great Palace monastery with four hundred monks sat in a circle. Each had a small velvet cushion on which to sit. They were all chanting quietly, but because there were so many, a hallowed reverberation of sound echoed around the Tibetan chamber.

Joshua, himself sat on a cushion with his eyes open at first, surveying the scene which had somehow unfolded before him and only a few weeks since Stanley had first mentioned the opportunity for him to visit this sacred place high in the Tibetan mountains.

After a while the monks all stopped chanting after a large hanging gold coloured gong was struck four times. The monks, each of them fell silent in unison. All entered a deep meditation, as did Joshua being used to this practise.

After an hour, the gong rang out loudly with a deep tone to its sound. The monks all quietly got up and left the room except for Sun Yin and Joshua who both remained seated as instructed earlier to do so by Sun Yin.

Sun Yin smiled, "How was that, Joshua?" enquired Sun Yin.

"I went very deep. I felt that I have been here many times before doing this myself, as a Tibetan monk here in a previous life-time," replied Joshua.

"Yes, yes. I was shown you doing that too. I knew from my own meditation and what I was shown was that you have indeed been a monk here in a previous life-time, Joshua. That is why the opportunity for this visit has occurred for you. In fact, I felt it beforehand even when Stanley phoned me a few weeks ago to see if you could come and visit us here. I was shown it in a dream just before, that a westerner fitting your description was due to visit us and here you are. This is not something we do for people who are not from Tibet," said Sun Yin.

"I understand," replied Joshua at the same time holding the palms of his hands together at chest height smiling at Sun Yin as he did so.

***

The next morning Joshua woke up early after a good night's sleep, despite the wind outside rattling the window's wooden shutters occasionally, this not being a surprise due to Lhasa being situated at nearly four-thousand metres above sea-level and with the palace above the city being built on a high rock escarpment.

A palace servant knocked at Joshua's bedroom door, "Come in," said Joshua.

The servant entered the room and gave Joshua a note from Sun Yin requesting him to be in the great hall at six-thirty a.m. dressed for a hike further up into the mountains. Joshua, duly carried out the instruction from Sun Yin.

Sun Yin greeted him in the great hall, where they could both eat breakfast and drink some coffee. Sun Yin looked Joshua in the eyes and said, "Joshua, I am sorry to wake you so early and without notice, but I felt today as the weather will be clear that I take you up on horseback, higher into the mountains to the highest monastery in the Himalaya, where a few of our monks live closest to heaven," Sun Yin laughing at his own words as he spoke them.

"Are you okay on horseback, Joshua?" continued Sun Yin.

"Yes, I think so," replied Joshua, somewhat tentatively.

"Good, we set off in an hour or so. Make sure you bring your warmest clothing. We will be staying the night in the monastery at the top of the world. I think you will find the experience interesting Joshua," said Sun Yin.

"Okay, I will make sure I am prepared," said Joshua, a bit surprised and still not quite awake, after being woken up early by the palace servant.

An hour later, Joshua wrapped up in his thick winter coat, met Sun Yin in the court-yard of the great Palace consisting of four-hundred rooms built in the seventh-century for a previous Dalai-Lama. The sky was clear and blue and the mountain air was crisp, a crescent moon still was visible low in the sky above the mountain tops.

Sun Yin was waiting already seated on his horse which looked well used to mountain hiking and well laden as it was so thick set and sturdy in size.

Joshua's horse was similar but smaller, just in case Joshua turned out not to be so good on the narrow mountain trails up the mountain.

"We have five miles upwards to go to the 'Monastery in the Sky,' it will take about half a day, as the trail is very narrow and dangerous!" said Sun Yin.

Joshua, mounted his horse, "Let's go," he said, adjusting his thick woollen hat.

The heavy gates of the Palace were opened and the horse's hooves echoed across the courtyard as they crossed the ancient cobble stoned square, an eagle was soaring high above them as they exited the Palace gates.

Eventually, the two men were out of the city and starting the climb up the mountain. There was silence except the howl of the wind through the mountain valley and the occasional shrill cry of the eagle soaring above them as if it was observing and guiding their journey ever higher towards the sky and the monastery above them.

"Tell me about this monastery, Sun Yin," Joshua asked, as the horses were walking diligently ever higher.

Sun Yin replied, "The monastery was built for a Dalai-Lama in the seventh century as a retreat for his own prayer and spiritual contemplation. He believed the higher up you were the better the quality of meditation and therefore the improvement of the spiritual wisdom of the seeker in question. That is why I am taking you there."

"I am looking forward to seeing it," replied Joshua.

"Good," replied Sun Yin.

Eventually they arrived at the monastery which seemed to be built into the cliff-side of the mountain. It was beautiful as the sun-light set upon it and lighting up the colour of the prayer flags and the revolving prayer wheels on the outer walls of the building.

As they arrived the same eagle which had followed them up the mountain gave out a shrill cry and soared ever higher leaving them as it did so, as if to say 'goodbye'.

'Welcome, Sun Yin," said another monk. He hugged Sun Yin close and smiled at him. They spoke in Tibetan, as Sun Yin explained his reason for taking Joshua high up the mountain to visit the monastery.

The other monk who could speak no English, only Tibetan, bowed to Joshua and he returned the gesture and bowed in front of the monk.

"This is Rinpoche Dachho, Joshua," said Sun Yin.

Joshua, shook his hand and said, "Nice to meet you Rinpoche Dachho," smiling as he spoke.

With that they were both escorted into the main room of the monastery where the ten monks who lived there spent so much of their own time in meditation.

"The monks here are even quieter and less predisposed to talking than normal monks. I know monks are usually quiet anyway. But the monks here have all come up here for a year from the main Palace Monastery. They have chosen to do this. It is akin to seclusion almost, even though there are always ten of them here. I spent a year up here myself, over twenty years ago for the same reason as them. This was to continue my own spiritual learning," said Sun Yin.

Joshua put down his small rucksack that he had taken with him up the mountain and had sat down in the middle of the main meditation room as Sun Yin had been speaking to him. Joshua had also noticed, that as the day was dry and clear and not freezing cold that the wooden shutters were all open wide allowing the clean crisp air to flood the building and that there was only one direction of view which was straight across to the Himalaya Mountains on the other side of the deep gorge below them and the sun was reflecting off the snow-covered peaks opposite them. Joshua at that point fully understood and appreciated why Sun Yin had taken him up to this monastery and rumoured to be the highest in the world, for it was truly breath-taking to his eyes.

"Stay here Joshua and meditate a while, while I check the horses are warm and okay in the stable next to the monastery. I will be back soon," said Sun Yin, he left Joshua alone in peace.

Joshua nodded and closed his eyes, he thought about all the times in his life that he had imagined being in such a place as the monastery high in the Himalaya Mountains, with wooden shutters, incense and statues of the Buddha all around him and that now he was in such a place. He listened intently – all he could hear was the wind whistling outside through the mountain pass below him and the faint sound of the hundreds of prayer-flags outside flapping in the wind. In a way, Joshua realised he did not even need to meditate, as the very situation he now found himself in, was the very kind of space he often visualized in his meditations to try to encourage his own inner spiritual development while meditating at home.

Joshua, felt a great surge of joy and gratitude for finding himself and the very people that enabled him this opportunity to be visiting Tibet.

***

That evening, after a heartening meal of rice and beans Joshua sat together with Sun Yin and the other monks in silence in the main room of the monastery. The wooden window shutters were now tightly closed to keep out the cold night air but with the wind still howling outside through the high mountain gorge and only a few feet away from where they sat the other side of the thick monastery stone walls. A snow storm outside had started and had turned into a fierce blizzard. A large log fire was alight and crackling in the open fireplace on the far side of the room, it was filled with the smell of incense sticks burning, at least a hundred candles flickered with light around the room. In one corner a large golden Buddha statue seemed to emit a powerful, yet serene peaceful energy. The atmosphere in the room used for their group meditation with the occasional chants of one monk at a time heightened the energy even more. Joshua, went deeper and deeper into his own meditation, an experienced meditator of many years practise thrived on the rich spiritual energy of the people present, all focused on their own spiritual growth as had indeed Joshua been so focused and for all his adult life.

In his meditation, Joshua found himself beside a stream where he met the Buddha, Jesus and the Swami-Baba whom he had visited in India, to each of them Joshua offered a question about that which troubled him most at that time. First, he asked the Buddha,

"Master how do I find peace in myself when a storm prevails within me?"

The Buddha replied, "Surrender your fears to God and trust all is well with the world and that things are as they should be in that moment. Be in your own present moment and there you will always find the peace that you require."

Joshua, in his mind then turned to Jesus and asked him, "Why are there crazy people ruling the most powerful countries on Earth now?"

To which Jesus replied, "In free countries, the consciousness of the leader reflects that of the people. For the leader to change, so the people must change in their own consciousness. Help to raise that consciousness through your own efforts and through the gifts available to you my son."

Finally, Joshua turned lastly to Swami-Baba and said, "Swami, I struggle so much with fearful and anxious thoughts, still mainly about my own health and the state of the world right now. What can I do to alleviate these thoughts?"

Swami-Baba replied, "Choose peace always. When you feel fear keep on choosing peace. Keep your focus always as much as possible on that which only brings you peace. Take your focus away from that which leads to fear within yourself. Keep choosing peace and you will emanate peace. In time, if enough of you do this peace will prevail. All will be well with the world in time. You will see. Trust, trust."

***

Joshua, opened his eyes and while still sat on his meditation cushion looked across the room at Sun Yin who was sat staring at him and smiling.

"Were you shown in your meditation something to help you at this time, Joshua?" he asked.

"Yes, I was Sun Yin. I was reminded yet again, to keep on choosing peace over anxiety or fear and to keep on remembering to do so in times of distress. It is good to be reminded of this, as it is so easy to forget at such times. I try to make it a habit to remember this," replied Joshua.

"Yes, yes," replied Sun Yin, nodding in agreement as the two men spoke. The rest of the monks present in the hall simply continued to sit and meditate in peace, the occasional chant coming from one of the monks at times.

The energy had built to a high level, the peace was almost audible. All that was truly audible though was the whistle and gusts of wind through the mountain pass outside a few feet from where they were sat. Even with the fire lit inside, the temperature inside the monastery was still low enough for their own breath to be visible.

Joshua said to Sun Yin, "I think I will retire for the night. I am very tired now."

"Of course, I will show you to your room," replied Sun Yin. Joshua, was taken to a small room with a low wooden framed bed with a thick woollen rug to use as a blanket, Joshua slept well on his first night in the monastery.

The next morning at breakfast, after another early meditation with the monks and Sun Yin, Joshua said to Sun Yin, "In my dreams last night, I dreamt that I was the eagle in the mountain valley, beside the monastery soaring high, but flying at night under the stars, when I guess the real eagle would have been resting."

"It is because you are connecting more with your own eagle energy now as you are here close to them, Joshua. The eagle reminds you of your quest for freedom from your own fears. You need to connect with that part of you, that allows this sense of freedom to prevail within you. The eagle comes to you in your dreams to show you this," said Sun Yin.

Joshua, smiled and nodded in agreement towards Sun Yin, but said only, "Yes" in reply.

The wooden shutters in the monastery were once again wide open to let the clear fresh mountain air percolate through the rooms of the ancient Tibetan cliff-side sanctity.

By now the snow had stopped falling and the air was crisp and the sky was deep blue and clear again. Joshua, looked out of the window. He saw what looked like the same eagle, which had seemed to follow them both up the mountain trail. It soared and turned on the air-currents in the mountain gorge below. The mountain eagle was a strong symbol for Tibetan's, as it is for the Native American Indians and representing freedom, strength and wisdom. To the tibetans it is also a symbol of spiritual growth of the soul of the individual and the main reason for Joshua's visit he thought to himself in visiting the magical land of Tibet.

***

The next few days were in essence, an intensive course in meditation, in an environment and place which Joshua had long dreamed of experiencing for himself and would often think while he was there that this was due to a recall of some previous Tibetan lifetime or other that he had once lived, so strong was his draw to Tibetan culture and it felt so familiar to him.

Joshua, reflected on something which had happened to him during his time at the monastery. One morning whilst engaged in his usual spiritual practise with the other monks, Joshua, found himself sat in a circle with the other ten inhabitants of the monastery, together with Sun Yin. Joshua, saw a vision appear in his mind. In the middle of the circle of the meditating monks a beautiful woman appeared of Native American appearance with long black platted hair. She was tall and slender in build and from her eyes a great outpouring of love was directed at Joshua and as their eyes met. The woman held out both arms towards him beckoning him forwards to join her. In his mind Joshua, stood up and went to her and the embrace she held out for him.

As they both held each other Joshua was overwhelmed by the love he felt for this woman in his heart. He could tell this love was a mutual feeling and that he seemed to know intuitively this beautiful Indian woman so well, as if he had known her all his life.

As they both embraced, Joshua was taken on a journey through time by this woman and who's inner beauty even eclipsed her own physical beauty. She was teaching Joshua some of the things about himself and his character that he had yet still to see clearly, about himself. She showed him the areas he doubted himself and how these self-doubts added to his list of fears in life. For despite Joshua's innate courage, he still regularly struggled with his own fears about having a shortage of money and fears about his own mortality, this despite his hard work in the spiritual arena of his own life.

The woman showed Joshua glimpses which she told him were glimpses of the future. She showed him a world changed by a viral pandemic spread around the globe affecting many people and of a warming of the planet which had been the choice of the world. She showed him a great migration of humanity from the hot areas of the Earth to the cooler ones for the survival of these people and all the upheavals this would cause to so many. She showed Joshua a massive revitalization of a strong spiritual belief in all that is good. She showed him how after a period of adjustment, that the people of the Earth, the environment and all living things, not only survived, but thrived after a great adjustment and a long period of many thousands of years of peace followed this change to the Earth.

The woman of great beauty showed Joshua that he was living during such times and the signs of change would begin to appear with ever increasing frequency within his own life-time.

She showed him, how using his own gifts, kindness and talents that he could help ease and facilitate the changes to come on Planet Earth along with many other people. Before the woman left Joshua, she showed him married to a strong and compassionate woman with a child that they would have together and who would grow up to be of great service to the world at large, but without elaborating further. She showed him that his relationship would not always be easy, like most relationships but that it was most important for his health and the wellbeing of his family to come, especially the child that they stay together and work through their problems and issues, otherwise the child also, would never fulfil her full potential in the world in terms of the many people she could help due to her special gifts. With that the beautiful Native American woman warmly embraced Joshua one final time and smiled at him as she slowly disappeared from Joshua's gaze. Joshua, came out of his deep meditation and wiped the tears from his eyes as he smiled to himself feeling a deep joy. He saw Sun Yin opposite him smiling back clasping his palms together gesturing, 'namaste'.

***

Joshua, through the course of his visit to the Palace in Lhasa and to the monastery high in the mountains he started to become aware of a subtle yet deep change within himself.

When males are growing up the assumption is that merely through reaching the age of eighteen years, is the age acknowledged as the time when male adults also make the passage into manhood. However, Joshua realised in himself and through observing many other males, that this was rarely the case. In fact, he believed many males never in fact make the transition to full manhood. Some native traditions would put their young men through various types of initiation processes, as they had an awareness of how important that this process was to encourage in men.

Joshua, knew that it was difficult to define. He knew even though he was in his mid-thirties in age that he had not quite made that full transition into manhood. It was only now due to his experiences, in part in the monastery high in the Himalaya that this 'flower' within was starting to bloom. Manhood had been awakened within himself, he only had this realisation because of the change within him. Had he not experienced this change within, he would have been none the wiser. He would like most males, just have assumed that he was a man because of his age. He realised how wrong he had been. Perhaps this transition into manhood is more visible to women, for some reason, Joshua thought to himself. Maybe, they knew all along whether a 'man' was a 'man', for some strange reason! In the same way, a man only 'truly' knows that he is a man, once he has made that transition.

The only other definition of what is required for the process to unfold, Joshua, thought to himself, was finding the courage within to face one's own fears. Perhaps, whatever was the greatest fear the individual suffered from and then to overcoming that fear and moving beyond it, adding that courage to 'oneself' making it easier to face each fear, as they presented within life.

Joshua, held his hands to his heart in the realisation of his change within himself. He knew that he had passed through his own initiations as they had presented themselves to him with his time spent in India, a journey he took alone at a time of personal sadness and with his hours spent in meditation with the monks in the monastery high on the mountain.

Sun Yin then spoke, "Joshua, a penny for your thoughts. I saw that you were deep in thought there. Has your visit up to this monastery helped you journey deeper into yourself?"

Joshua replied, "Yes, it has. I was just thinking that exactly, Sun Yin. I felt as if only very recently I have shifted into 'manhood' on a deeper level within myself. I cannot put my finger on one thing which has brought the change about or has encouraged the shift. Maybe, it's just through me facing more of my own fears I guess! About illness, death, being alone, feeling unloved. Those sorts of things, I suppose. I definitely feel different to how I was before."

"Yes, I understand that too. I remember going through something similar too. You know you have become a different person inside to who you were before. It is not just about being more mature. You actually, feel like a different person. More confident and less afraid," said Sun Yin.

"Exactly that. Exactly that, you're right, Sun Yin. And you feel more of a man, in part because of the journey that you have made within your own self and the things, often, your greatest fears that you have had to face and survived," replied Joshua.

"Yes, you have grown. You are a new person. You have passed through one of the 'valleys of death'. There are several," said Sun Yin.

Joshua replied, "I think Sun Yin, it is part of the process of waking up to who we all are at the deepest level. At our core. Which is a spirit in a physical body and yet connected to the 'Spirit of the World'."

"Yes, yes. We are that exactly: 'The spirit of the World'," replied Sun Yin.

***

The next morning Joshua and Sun Yin said their goodbyes to the other monks and saddled up their horses for their trek back down part of the mountain from the 'sky high' monastery to return to the Potala Palace in Lhasa far below them, the eagle following their passage as they wound their way back down the mountain trail again it seemed to Joshua and who could not stop staring at the bird of prey as well as fixating on the magnificence of the mountain scenery all around him.

Both men were well wrapped up in their thick winter woollen coats and hats to keep out the wind and cold even though the sun was shining it was still very cold due to the high altitude and strong winds which so often blew through the mountain pass all the way back down to Lhasa – a city located at a staggering four thousand metres above sea-level. The two men spent most of the few hours on horse-back back down to the Palace in silence, Joshua, reflecting on all that his time in relative solitude with the monks, meditating and about what he had learned about himself and others from the experience.

Sun Yin, simply being mainly in the moment. When they arrived back at the Dalai-Lama's Palace in Lhasa, the massive heavy wooden gates were already open for them. The horse's hooves echoed back across the pebbles as they walked now slow and tired towards their stables on the far side of the courtyard. There they were met by one of the monks who escorted the horses to a much-needed meal and rest.

"Hello, Joshua, welcome back Sun Yin," said the young monk.

"It is good to be back," Joshua replied. Sun Yin just smiled at the monk.

The following day was to be Joshua's day on which he would begin his journey back home to England.

Sun Yin said to him, "Joshua, this evening after we have rested, we will meet at seven p.m. in the great hall for a last meal before your return tomorrow."

"Okay, I am ready for a rest now too," replied Joshua.

Later, that evening the two friends met in the great hall for a last supper together and to discuss Joshua's stay at the Palace.

Sun Yin said to him, "So, Joshua, what do think has been most useful that you have learnt here during your visit?"

Joshua paused to reflect briefly and replied, "To trust myself: my true self, in each moment of my life and to surrender my fears to God when they encroach on my being."

"Yes, good," said Sun Yin smiling.

Of course, Joshua had learnt much more than this, but in that moment, his brief reply was sufficient for Sun Yin. Both knew that they had each learnt more about themselves and life, even Sun Yin who was older and wiser.

Both men realised life was an ongoing journey of learning about their own true nature.

***

The last night at the Palace as he slept, Joshua had a dream in which Papa Luca came to him, they both spoke, Papa Luca however in the dream was dressed as a Tibetan Buddhist monk with cropped grey hair, even though in the dream and in his soul Joshua knew it was Papa Luca who presented himself in this manner and dressed in such an attire yet so relevant to Joshua's location, of course. In the dream, Papa Luca gave Joshua some answers to some of his struggles and both men transformed into mountain eagles and soared on the thermal mountain air high up into the snowy mountain peaks. As they did so Joshua could feel more deeply and intimately than ever before a sense of oneness and surrender with the world. The sense of trust that the eagle had that it's next meal would always be presented somewhere in nature to help sustain its life without fear of its own survival. He knew in his soul, that as the eagle he did not fear death either, for the eagle had no concept of death because the eagle was too immersed in its own concept of being at one with the Earth in each moment. It was as if the eagle did not have any awareness of the future, or of any negativity it could hold as the magnificent bird of prey.

As he flew as the eagle, the eagle that was his friend Papa Luca flew beside him. Joshua, knew instinctively that his friend somehow was a part of his dreams unfoldment.

In his dream, later Joshua found himself to be a Tibetan monk also sat with Papa Luca in the Palace monastery in Lhasa. Papa Luca was speaking to him in his own mind. He showed him how he did not physically have to travel in his human form to such magnificent or enchanting places to secure the spiritual revelations he and so many others sought in their lives, places that they thought they needed to go to physically to capture and return with the answers of the mysteries they sought in their hearts and minds. Though, this in truth could seem to be more of an adventure it was not a requirement to seek such answers.

Instead, Papa Luca in his dream showed him that he could travel, in his dreams, his meditations, his imagination and discover all the answers - in the inner universe of his being. He was shown how he, as are all people, connected to the ocean of the world, the ocean of the universe. That as much as they were a part of it, they also ultimately, were all of it. All of 'all that is'. The imagination of each person was their own passport to all the answers. 'Ask and you will be shown,' Joshua remembered on his awakening from his dream!

***

Joshua, woke up early on his last morning at the Potala Palace in Lhasa. He flung open the wooden shutters, and looked out across the city. The city was already coming to life. Smoke was circling up into the sky from the domestic fires burning to heat the small houses in the distance below the Palace with signs of life of the day's commencement in the crisp clean mountain air. The sky had its usual deep blue colour and the snow was sparkling in the early sun off the mountain's snow covered surface.

Joshua, reflected briefly about the dream from the previous night and he smiled to himself and thought about how Papa Luca even had some mysterious pass into his dreams as well as his random appearances in his real everyday life, be it his haunt, at the galley Café in his home town by the sea.

Joshua, quickly got dressed, the rest of his belongings having been packed the previous evening in preparation for his homeward journey. He went down to the main hall where Sun Yin was waiting for him already dressed in his usual manner - his purple monks robe. He smiled at Joshua, with a touch of sadness in his eyes and said,

"Joshua, you are leaving us. I will miss you a great deal. We have discovered more about ourselves in the short time of your visit. I hope that I have taken you to places where you have made a journey more deeply into your own soul of self-discovery?"

"Indeed, you have!" Joshua replied, with compassion, love and sadness in his eyes too.

"I will never forget my stay here," he continued, trying to fight back his own tears. Sun Yin gave Joshua a small package of home cooked Tibetan food, tightly wrapped in grease-proof paper and tied with a thick coarse piece of string.

"For your journey home!" he said.

"Thank you," replied Joshua, smiling back at him.

With the words of farewell over Joshua left the Palace for his long journey home.

***

A month had passed back home for Joshua, life had returned to its normal routine. He would often reflect on his time in Tibet, his stay in the Potala Palace and his days spent higher still in the Himalaya's, in the mountain monastery and his time spent with the monks and Sun Yin meditating for much of the time that he spent there, the icy wind howling beyond the thick wooden shutters, and the eagles drifting on the wind high in the sky.

By this time though the memory was of course still clear, but the experience itself already had started to feel part of a past-life experience somehow, even though only a month had passed since his return.

Joshua, walked down the High Street of his home town, he decided to go the Galley Café for his breakfast. The surf-boards were still on the walls and hanging from the ceiling as they were before his Tibetan experience.

As he entered the café, he said, "Hello" to the owner and took a seat by the window and ordered his breakfast. No sooner had he started to eat, in walked his old friend Papa Luca.

"Hello Joshua, how was your trip to Lhasa?" said Papa Luca, smiling from ear to ear.

"Amazing, it would appear even in Tibet that you could find me somehow!" replied Joshua.

Papa Luca, still smiling through his thick grey beard, replied, "Ah, by that you must mean our meeting in the dream. When I appeared, also, as a Tibetan monk, even though your soul still recognised me. Didn't you?"

Joshua, looked at Papa Luca smiling back at him as well, "Yes, how did you know about my dream?" he asked.

"Because, I was in it too. I am aware of my dreams too you know. I wanted to join you there. I was envious. So, I joined you there in my own lucid dream. Can you dream at will Joshua?" replied Papa Luca.

"I cannot bring about a dream to order. No, I cannot," replied Joshua looking disappointed as he answered.

"One day you will," said Papa Luca still smiling.

Papa Luca ordered his coffee and sat down to join Joshua at his table. They spoke for an hour or more with Joshua relaying much of his experiences and his insights from his trip.

During this hour, Papa Luca remained entirely silent, listening intently only to Joshua and his relay of his time spent at the two monasteries in Tibet and about his time spent with Sun Yin.

After Joshua had finished speaking, Papa Luca spoke,

"It would seem that one of the things you have learnt from your trip is how the mind is like walking a tight-rope. It can, we all know, be so difficult not to become immersed in our thoughts, fearful ones or otherwise. Irrespectively, they of course keep us from being truly present, truly present in the present moment. That place which is the point of power within ourselves. The only place that we can be in the full presence of the life force, or God, or whatever you wish to call it! All the teachings, the methods, the practises, are to help us to develop the awareness and the ability to develop the consciousness, to keep as much as possible our awareness in the present moment. That is life's greatest challenge. Otherwise in truth we do not really live. We just exist in our minds eye instead!

When we have learnt to truly do this, we will have mastered our thought and emotions. They no longer are the master of us. Don't you think so, Joshua?"

Joshua, paused for a moment and then replied,

"Yes, you are right. It is so often, so difficult. Our fears, our worries and our thoughts, keep on stealing the moment from us – if we let them. It is like walking a tight-rope to stay in the present moment I find. Practise. More practise. Self-awareness is required."

Papa Luca listened carefully to Joshua's reply. Then he replied, "Yes, it is for us all to keep remembering that we are not the mind. That we are not the body, we are not our thoughts. We are each of us, divine, pristine consciousness. All part of the ocean of consciousness of all creation. That is what we all really are. The essence of that and us all therefore, as well as the essence of love and peace. We can return, back to that in each moment, if we choose in our hearts and minds to do so. The trick, is to keep on always remembering to do that whenever we so require."

"I try to remember. I try to do that. I keep on forgetting I have a choice. Some worry or fear, usually in my case about my own health and wellbeing, keeps on returning like a thief in the night and stealing my peace, or so it often seems," said Joshua.

"Remember, always you have the power to return to peace and love in yourself. Remember and make that your habit Joshua," replied Papa Luca. Joshua, smiled back at him.

Papa Luca finished his coffee, bid Joshua farewell and once again seemed to disappear into the crowds on the street outside.

***

After Papa Luca had left the Galley Café, Joshua ordered another pot of tea and began to reflect on his travels and adventures over the recent months. He thought about his time spent in India and his most recent adventure in the mountains of Tibet. He realised how lucky he was to have the good health, time, freedom and money to be able to do so. He knew that at some stage he might get married and have children too, that being one of life's expectations and a great adventure in a different way. An adventure that is marriage and would involve much personal sacrifice and focus, shifting to others, rather than himself. In so doing, he thought to himself, that would reduce his own introspection which often converged on worry, that being the type of introspection he never now really enjoyed. He was now most happy when his mind was free of any thoughts.

He looked at the emerald and diamond gold ring on his right hand that Swami had miraculously manifested before his very eyes, and then presented to him with as a gift. The ring was something so many people on their own visits to see Swami-Baba often wished to receive. What they wished for even more was their personal transformation or some healing or other for another person close to them.

Joshua, realised the ring was special to him though not because of how he got it but because of what it symbolised to him personally. In the centre was a square emerald made up of four small green emerald stones and when he looked at these stones it reminded him of the colour of the heart energy chakra and that he should focus there when he felt his heart was shut off for whatever temporary reason. When he looked at the two engraved Cobra heads facing in towards the emerald, with their diamond encrusted heads, it reminded him of the challenges in life of how they can induce fear and yet those experiences hold the diamonds of wisdom through encountering them and the growth such brings. Finally, it reminded him of how through the emeralds colour of the heart chakra, the symbol of the love that is impregnable to the power of fear and that being the saviour of each soul when they remember to return their focus back to love at times of great personal difficulty. Joshua also thought what would it be like and to have evolved sufficiently that in one instant he could be able to manifest such a thing. Joshua, had learnt already through the course of his life that such things were indeed possible, for he had witnessed it himself. He knew that all people have the power to manifest or to bring things and people into their lives, just that they don't realise when it happens and that they did it themselves, through the power of their own thoughts, focus and actions over a period of time. To manifest a ring, he wondered was it just about knowing and believing, without any doubt at all – then it could be done in an instant, even by himself, maybe?"

***

Several months had passed since Joshua had arrived back home from his trip to Tibet. He had not even seen Papa Luca for weeks, he thought to himself. His life had settled back into its usual routine of living alone and in the small town by the sea. Each day Joshua would see the same familiar faces of the local inhabitants and who he had seen like himself, slowly aging with the passage of time despite his relative youthfulness in years. He often wished to see more new faces around the place, but still he enjoyed the sense of community and belonging that comes with living in a small community town even though it had a regular influx of tourists in the holiday season.

Joshua would reflect on the state of the world's problems of one type and another which seemed to be steadily increasing all the time causing so much anxiety and distress among so many people and in so many parts of the world that he felt at such times even more grateful for his relative isolation compared to many from the abundance of such modern-day problems, though he was in truth as connected to them as anyone else but often didn't realise the fact it was so.

Joshua, knew he could only do so much to improve the state of the world. He wished he could do more about it and wondered how he might do so. One of Joshua's means of making a living was writing, fiction and maybe one day he could use his skill to help somehow with these sorts of problems that the world faced.

***

Joshua, decided it was time for another trip, another adventure. He remembered a friend of his, Mark who lived in a town called Glastonbury had given him the name of the son of a tribal medicine man on a Native American Indian Reservation in Taos, New Mexico in the United States of America. Joshua decided on a whim to book a ticket and made a reservation in a local hotel there three weeks hence. Joshua was impulsive by nature!

Before his trip to America, he decided that he would visit his friend Mark for the first time in months in Glastonbury. He knew where Mark always went for a coffee in the town and arranged to meet him there the next day.

The next day he duly arrived at the coffee shop as arranged.

"Hello, Joshua. Good to see you again. It's been a long-time mate!" said Mark.

Mark, himself was about sixty years old, his hair was grey and had fully receded and he tied back what was left in a ponytail. He was often sat in the café there at the same table doing his psychic readings, which is how they both had originally met when Joshua happened to be going through a break-up with a girlfriend he had at the time.

Joshua replied, "Yes, it's been a while Mark, how are you?"

"Very well thanks, Joshua. I hear that you are planning a trip to see my friend 'Standing Elk' in Taos New Mexico?" Mark replied.

"Yes, how did you know. I have not told anyone yet?" Joshua replied, with a quizzical look on his face.

"It's in the cards of course," replied Mark smiling.

A set of tarot cards were set out on the table in front of him.

"Sit down, I will give you a free reading! If you want one, that is?" said Mark and still smiling.

"Okay, that would be fascinating. Your readings are always accurate!" Joshua replied, with a big grin on his face. He sat down and Mark asked him to pick out six cards from the pack and place them on the table in front of them both. Mark studied the cards for a short time as his friend waited hesitantly for his reply.

Mark said, "I see that you have been travelling a lot lately. You have made trips far away to seek answers about yourself and to many of life's mysteries, have you not?"

"Yes, I have," replied Joshua.

Mark continued doing the reading, without looking up he continued to examine the cards and to see what they were trying to tell him and to help his friend.

Mark said, "I see you as I already said, taking a trip very soon to the United States to a Native American Indian Reservation. I see you meeting up with my friend 'Standing Elk' of whom I told you about previously. He will help you further on your journey, deeper into your own soul and spirit. He will be able to help you further with your initiation into manhood. You are almost there! But there is a skill, that he will be able to unlock for you Joshua. That will be the power of manifestation. You have sought this ability for a long time. He will help you achieve this. You know this is only the first stop.

You know the world is in a dark place now with so many problems with the climate and the environment and people's anxieties about it all, like many others do also. You cannot do it all! But, you have a great skill. You can write well and pass on your wisdom to many others to help them also unlock their own talents and skills to help them also to go out into the world to help others do their work. It will be a very enriching trip Joshua. You must go!"

"Thank you, Mark," replied Joshua, giving him ten pounds and smiling as he did so.

"Thanks. Good luck," Mark replied.

Joshua bid his friend farewell and left the café. He went up to the famous Glastonbury Tor, once he arrived at the top he felt gratitude in his heart for the message received from Mark's card reading. He thought about his forthcoming journey to meet Standing Elk and what he hoped would be his next spiritual adventure. He wondered too about what it in turn it might lead to and how he could best help others make the world a better and safer place!

***

The plane landed in Albuquerque, after a transfer flight via Denver. Taos, was seventy miles or so north and just passed Santa Fe, the capitol of the state of New Mexico in the United States and a ski resort in winter as was Taos. Joshua, was visiting in May however and the only person that he knew of there through the recommendation of Mark, was 'Standing Elk', the son of the local medicine-man.

Standing Elk had spoken to Mark and having heard of Joshua's visit said that he would be pleased to meet

Joshua during his visit to Taos which was close to the Reservation.

Joshua, arrived at the square in Taos, a small dusty town, twenty or so miles passed Santa Fe. He booked himself into an old hotel in the town's square.

"Do you know standing Elk?" Joshua asked the receptionist at the hotel, an elderly woman who looked Mexican to him.

"Yes, of course, everyone here knows Standing Elk!" the receptionist replied.

"I am hoping to meet him during my stay at some point. A friend of mine in England knows him and said that I should look him up," Joshua said sheepishly not wishing to sound too strange to the woman.

"You will find him, Taos is a small place. Most mornings he is at the Corral Café, with his blonde girlfriend. I am sure you will find him there one morning, this week at least," the receptionist replied.

"Great, thanks for your help," replied Joshua as he walked out of the hotels main door into the bright sunshine and facing out onto the small square, in the small town in what felt to him as the middle of know-where. Joshua hoped he would get to meet Standing Elk, as it was, after all, his main reason for his visit. However, in his mind there was no particular reason. His friend Mark had mentioned his friendship with him, but also Joshua had been strangely given a book for free by a book-shop owner he knew in his home town about artists inspired by the landscape around the town of Taos and its surrounding area. Joshua noticed coincidences and synchronicities and often acted upon them, as he had learned from past experiences that there was often a reason and a purpose to them.

Joshua, spent a few days in the town getting used to his new environment, it was so different to his home town by the sea in England. Instead of horses, being the main mode of transport in the old western town, as they once were long ago, Joshua, noticed many people used motorcycles for getting around and without having to legally wear a helmet, unlike back home. He noticed how so many cars, battered and dented from use, had no rust on them, due to the dry air in this arid region, even though the town was several thousand feet above sea-level on a vast plain.

Joshua, on one of his walks around the town spotted the Corral Café mentioned to him by the receptionist at his hotel. Sure enough, he spotted a man of obvious Native American appearance, his hair slightly greying and pulled back into a ponytail. He was wearing a black leather bomber jacket covered in various stitched-on motorcycle badges, some blue Levi jeans and a pair of cowboy boots. Sat next to him as expected was an attractive blonde woman, as foretold by the hotel receptionist.

Joshua, approached them both, slightly nervously unaware of the reception he might get and being a total stranger to them. Joshua said, "Hello, my name is Joshua, I am a friend of Mark in Glastonbury, England. He told me that you are a friend of his too. Is your name Standing Elk?"

The man replied, "Of course, Bro, good to meet you. Mark sent me an email, a while back about you coming over, I remember it! He said you were on some sort of spiritual journey looking for 'answers'. How can I help you Bro? Take a seat. Do you want a drink?"

"Sure, thanks. I'll have a coffee please," replied Joshua. He sat down and his new acquaintance bought him a coffee and re-joined them both.

"How was your trip over? Is it your first time in the U.S. Bro?" asked Standing Elk.

"No, I have spent a week in New York before," replied Joshua.

"So, why Taos now Bro?" he asked.

"I was led here by a trail of coincidences and I felt I had to come. I am not sure of the reason. Mark, knowing you was a part of that and after he mentioned that he knew you, I thought I should look you up. For some reason, I feel a strong affinity with Native American Indian culture and about how they once lived in the past so in tune with nature. I think that I was one, once in a previous life-time, I guess. In a funny sort of way, I even miss that way of life - how they lived back then I mean," replied Joshua.

"I get that, how can I help you though Bro?" replied Standing Elk, looking at Joshua quizzically.

"I don't know. Tell me, if you don't mind, what is it like to be a Native American Indian living in this country now?" Joshua replied as politely as he could.

"It is shit! This is not our best time. Little work, lots of alcoholism, little money. There is little pride amongst many of us. Many feel like second class citizens still. Life is a struggle. One day we hope that there will be big changes and that someday we will once again be freer to express ourselves and that we will be heard more. This is our country, it always was and it always will be! Everyone else is an immigrant. Whatever generation they are as far as I am concerned. Does that answer your question Bro?" replied Standing Elk.

"Yes, it does. I am not surprised to hear you say that. I can tell you are angry but that is understandable bearing mind what has happened to your people here in the last few centuries," replied Joshua.

"Wouldn't you be, if you were in my shoes Bro?" replied Standing Elk.

"Yes, I would be angry too," replied Joshua.

This beautiful woman is called Linda by the way. Sorry, I didn't introduce you to her earlier," he said smiling at them both as he spoke.

"Nice to meet you Linda," said Joshua as he shook her hand. Linda's bright blue eyes radiated an inner wisdom he could tell that she did not takes fools gladly.

"We have to go now Bro, we have an appointment. We can talk more tomorrow if you like? We can pick you up here at the same time and if you like we can take you for a visit to our Reservation and my house there. I know that you would like to meet my father who is the local medicine man, because Mark told me!" said Standing Elk.

"That would be great. I will see you tomorrow then," replied Joshua with a broad smile. The couple left and Joshua sat and reflected on the meeting as he continued to drink his coffee.

The next day Standing Elk turned up in an old battered blue van. Joshua, was already waiting standing outside the Corral Café.

"Jump in," said Standing Elk and so Joshua got into the van.

"So, how long have you had this fascination for our Indian culture then?" asked Standing Elk.

"Oh, for as long as I remember. Certainly, since I got more interested in the spiritual side of life and since I was a teenager. I meditate regularly and stuff and I have been on trips recently to India and Tibet to learn more about spirituality. I guess in no small part, because of those visits they have somehow led me here too and to continue my journey of spiritual exploration and I know that in your culture that there is a long tradition of such," replied Joshua.

"Yes, it would be fair to say that. I am interested in your trips to India and Tibet. That sounds a blast! My father is always trying to teach me spiritual stuff, but it is only in recent years that I have started to take notice of him. For so much of my life I was so angry with the white man, that I just got drunk and chased women. I have changed in recent years. Something happened to me. I had an out-of-body experience during which I was shown how I was on the wrong path. I was shown that if I carried on as I was that as well as bringing much suffering to others, as well as myself, that I would not live to be an old man.

Since then I have started to listen more to my father. I know he is very wise. His Indian name is White Eagle Feather," said Standing Elk.

The van pulled off the highway onto what seemed like poor scrub-land. Dotted about the land were small humble homesteads, some with vehicles parked outside, otherwise with little signs of life. There were no signs of wealth on the Reservation, or the 'Res' for short, as Standing Elk and others referred to it!

The van stopped outside one of the houses. They both got out of the vehicle and Joshua was invited inside. In the house were several large brightly painted canvases hung on the wall.

"They are all my paintings. Native American Indian art, if you want to call it that I suppose Joshua. It is heavy with influences of my culture, as you can tell.

Eagles, western landscapes and stuff as you can see for yourself," said Standing Elk proudly.

"Yes, I can see that. I like it a lot. I think that you are a very talented artist," replied Joshua, still looking at the paintings on the walls of the room.

"Thank you, Bro," replied Standing Elk.

The door creaked open at that moment and in walked an older Indian man, about seventy-five years of age.

"This is my father, White Eagle Feather. Dad, this is Joshua," Standing Elk said, smiling at Joshua as he spoke.

The medicine man looked at Joshua but did not smile. He did not hold out his hand to him. Then he spoke softly and calmly, "This is in my lifetime only the second time a white-man has entered our house, so you are honoured that my son has brought you here. It was your friend Mark from England who also visited us here a couple of years ago. He and Standing Elk were brothers in a previous lifetime.

You are welcome, if my son has brought you here too. I had a dream only last night that a westerner would be visiting me soon and who I must teach the wisdom I should share. I was told this person in the future would write books about his experiences which would help many people around the world. I can say now to you that this person is you! I recognise you from my dream. You are in part because of that, most welcome. Take a seat. Can we get you a drink Joshua?" said White Eagle Feather.

"That would be nice. I am not sure what to say now? I have never even thought about writing a book! Maybe, I will in the future at some point. Anyway, I just go with the flow I suppose, when I am not worrying about something or other. My worries keep on stealing the moment away from me, which is frustrating to say the least," said Joshua.

"Your thoughts are merely like clouds that cross the sky. Observe them, just don't get attached to them. They come and go. The real you is there always, the eternal silent witness inside of you. Inside of all of us! That is the great spirit or 'Wakan Tanka' as we often call God," said the medicine man.

"Yes, I agree. It is just that I find trying to stay in the moment is a bit like trying to balance on a tight-rope," replied Joshua.

"Yes, it is, but that is the skill you must learn if you wish to be a master of yourself and your emotions. They must not rule you. You must learn to rule them. Show them who is chief!" said White Eagle Feather.

Standing Elk gave Joshua a cup of coffee.

"Thank you," said Joshua.

White Eagle Feather continued to speak, "Life is hard here, as I am sure you can see. The white man stole our lands across this vast country and in return gave us small patches of scrub land with no resources below its surface. We still must fight a lot of racial prejudice to get anything, so we remain poor.

However, there is a change in the world. Many see it now. There is much pain and suffering. The white man is learning that they must respect the planet and all cultures, otherwise humanity itself, will not survive!"

"Yes, I agree. There have been many signs in the last twenty years or so especially, which prove this to be the case. Do you think that humanity will survive all the upheaval that the world is in right now?" Joshua asked White Eagle Feather.

He replied, "Yes, but there is still much suffering until humanity turns the corner towards this brighter future.

Joshua, I would like to take you up into the mountains nearby, to show you something I feel in my spirit because I can tell, in fact I know in my heart your soul is Native American Indian. It is so strong in you that I feel that you are one of us, even though I have only just met you!

High on the mountain is a spot where young Indian men are taken to undergo a spiritual initiation. Do you feel ready. There must be no fear. That is the sign that you are ready for such an initiation?" said White Eagle Feather.

"I am not afraid. So, I guess that means that I am ready. I was not expecting anything from you, I might add," replied Joshua.

"Yes, I know you didn't. This came from my dream. I was instructed in my dream to take you to this place upon your visit to our house. That is why I make this offer to you now. Do you accept this offer?"

"Yes, of course," replied Joshua.

"Come then," Joshua followed White Eagle Feather, while Standing Elk remained in the house, for he knew the tradition, that when an elder took another Indian for a 'spiritual initiation', they always went alone, unless it was at the request of the Medicine Man. For then and only then, would the Medicine Man be a guide through what was to come!

***

Joshua and White Eagle Feather, the tribal medicine man, climbed into the old Ford pick-up truck parked outside the house and drove off up the mountain trail.

White Eagle Feather spoke as he drove up the trail, "Joshua, I was shown in my dream that you visited 'Wakan Tanka' in his human form in the East. Do you know how privileged you were to have had such an auspicious opportunity as that?"

"I know that it was a blessing. That is all. I am not sure I can fully comprehend what it means in the greater scope of things. At the time I went, I carried much sadness deep inside about some personal issues. Amongst other things, it helped me through some of that, then and since. Since then I have also spent time in two monasteries' in Tibet with some monks. I learnt a lot there too," replied Joshua.

White Eagle Feather said nothing further. He just smiled at Joshua and continued the drive up the mountain trail. A few minutes later after White Eagle Feather had spoken, for some reason Joshua started to feel anxious. He wondered what the elderly Indian was going to put him through during the initiation which lay ahead of him.

White Eagle Feather, could now sense Joshua's agitation. The medicine man spoke after his spell of silence.

"Joshua, what you fear now is the reason that I am taking you to this location. High up here in the mountain is a secret and sacred site to which the white men are not allowed access. My son and I can feel the energy of your Native American Indian ancestry still inside your spirit. Within you there is the spirit of the eagle, within you now, waiting to lead your soul, your spirit on to do what you came here to do in this life. I will help you make that contact, that connection with the eagle's power."

Joshua, did not reply, he just looked White Eagle Feather briefly in the eyes. They drove on up the mountain passing the tree-line and leaving a trail of dust in the vehicles wake. The sun was starting to set and an amber coloured light filled the western sky.

Eventually, they reached their destination and got out of the vehicle and walked a short distance to a clearing a short way from the edge of the high mountain ridge. They could see below them, the Reservation and the town beyond. Stretched out in front of them they could see for over seventy miles across the high flat plain passed Sante Fe and beyond. White Eagle Feather found some brush wood and began to light a small fire and they both sat with their legs crossed on the bare ground and stared into the fire as it started to burn brighter and brighter as they did so White Eagle Feather started to chant and then sing in his Tiwa tribes language. As he did so, he waved a piece of burning sage around them both to help clear the space and their own energy fields.

After fifteen minutes or so, of chanting the medicine man went silent and started to meditate and Joshua did the same instinctively. Joshua, went deep into the own silence of his own being, he saw a white Eagle soaring high above him in his mind's eye and he himself became an Eagle too in his own mind and followed the other Eagle. They seemed to fly back through time side by side back to Joshua's past life as a Tiwa Indian living at the nearby Pueblo which had stood for hundreds of years. He saw himself married to his wife and he saw his children too. He saw that he himself had come to be both chief of the tribe, hundreds of years earlier and a man greatly revered by the elders. He saw then in his mind why the synchronicities had led him to Taos and why White Eagle Feather and his son Standing Elk had been gracious enough to welcome him, not only to their home on the Reservation but also to bring him to the special location usually out of bounds to the white man, even in this modern age. Joshua, felt a great love for the people and the tribe he no longer knew as a westerner from another country and the culture of his current life-time.

The two Eagles flew across the mighty oceans and he saw in a glimpse what had unfolded in India and Tibet relative to his visits. He even recognised himself as the Eagle he watched as he and Sun Yin took the path up the Tibetan mountain trail there to visit the highest monastery, one of the few left after the years of destruction by a people who did not see with the eyes of the clarity of the Eagles spirit. During the flight as the Eagle, Joshua felt a strange sensation of change in his own spirit, deep within his soul. Rather than a surge of strength there was a release of a fear he could not identify exactly, but he felt it was to do with that life as the Indian Chief.

The Eagle took him back to the Pueblo, to another life there as a young Indian about twenty years of age, who had a strong love for his wife and a member of the tribe. He saw himself get sick and die and he realised in that life there was much emotional pain because he did not wish to leave his wife because of the intensity of his love for her. That death had left within him a memory of death that haunted him and left within his soul a residue of fearing death and illness. He could see now where that fear was born. He could also now, see through this insight that the same fear had left his own being. He saw then this was the initiation, the gift, that the Eagle meditation and the initiation with White Eagle Feather had taken him through was.

With that realisation, Joshua came out of his meditation – White Eagle Feather was sat opposite him in the darkness but for the dim light of the fires embers smouldering in front of them both in the crisp night air. Beyond the stars shone high above them and passed the mountain peak, a full moon shone brightly high in the sky. Joshua, felt lighter and the weight he had carried for many life-times before this one had flown away. The two men smiled at each other now with a much greater acknowledgement. They drove back down the mountain trail in silence back to the house on the Reservation they had left a few hours earlier.

***

Joshua, and White Eagle Feather, arrived back at the Reservation and they both knew that the work they had both needed to do was now complete. Joshua shook their hands and said goodbye to Standing Elk and White Eagle Feather.

On his way, back to England Joshua had decided to visit New York City, a place he had always wished to visit and so he had prearranged a brief visit to his old friend Jim, who had once also lived in the same sea-side town and where they had both become good friends several years earlier.

Joshua, arrived in New York not only excited to visit this great metropolis but also pleased to be able to spend time with his old friend.

"Hi, great to see you Joshua," said Jim and beaming a big smile at him at the JFK arrivals exit point.

"Hi, Jim, how are you? We have so much to catch up on," replied Joshua.

"We do man. It is so great to see you. I can't wait to hear about your recent trips man. You've been all over the place on some weird spiritual quest! But, you always were into all that stuff, I remember from when I lived in England near you. That is when I was sober enough to remember," replied Jim laughing.

Joshua started to laugh too and they both hugged each other warmly. They caught one of the iconic yellow taxi's back into the city from the airport and chatting all the while, both reminiscing about their times in the old sea-side town and about Joshua's trips to India, Tibet and the most recent one to the Reservation in New Mexico.

Joshua, kept on staring at the sea of lofty sky-scrapers almost touching the sky. He could feel the vibe of the city, even though it was daylight in the city that never sleeps.

Jim was about forty years of age and like many people had not had an easy life after having been brought up by his older sister from his early teenage years after both of his parents had died. He carried still, much pain and sadness of his loss and alcohol was one of his methods to help him cope with that pain. When Jim was sober, Joshua, found him great company. When Jim was drunk, well, that was a different story!

"So, Jim remind me again, how and why you came to live in New York and how did you get a green card to help you stay and work here?" Joshua asked.

Jim was silent for a while as the taxi drove into the city and as the traffic flowed through it like a colony of ants, yet insulated from the noise outside. Then Jim replied, "I arrived a few years ago. I had no plan. I stayed first on a friend's couch in the Bronx. He kicked me out after a couple of weeks. Then for six months, including my first winter here, I slept rough on the streets and in a van I bought cheaply!"

Joshua, looked at Jim in silent disbelief.

Jim continued, "It was tough to say the least. I saw all sorts of shit, but I met many people with many stories. Mostly sad ones. Eventually, I made friends with someone who hired fake guns for when they made either movies or television series in the city which required them. I was his general dogs-body. I did all sorts of weird stuff.

I started getting paid and eventually started earning enough money to pay my rent and start to live. Of course, it was a great relief to be not sleeping on the streets. The winters are so cold here!

Now I feel a part of this city man. There are people from all over the world living here, working, earning money. Sometimes a lot of money. I just live day to day. You never know what is around the corner, do you?"

"No, you don't Jim. I can't believe you lived on the street for that first winter though! I bet you could write a book about that alone, couldn't you?" said Joshua.

"I could, but I wouldn't want to relive it now though!" replied Jim.

"I guess so," said Joshua.

Soon after both friends got out of the taxi and Jim took Joshua to his room. It was in a downtown rough part of the city but it would be free accommodation for Joshua and he was just grateful to save some money for once!

Jim said, "Let's go out and get something to eat. I know a great restaurant downtown on Broadway Joshua, fancy it?"

Joshua replied, "Great, I am hungry. I didn't eat on the plane during my flight here from Albuquerque."

"Let's go then," said Jim.

The two men left the basic sparse accommodation and went out into the bustling city streets, out into a cacophony of noise and people rushing in all directions too busy with their own thoughts and lives to notice anyone else and the way so many live whether in city's or not, Joshua thought to himself.

The two men sat down in the restaurant and as it was still early ordered a plate of pancakes with maple syrup and a large coffee each. The restaurant was popular and with its share of tourists as it sometimes had singing waiters and waitresses to entertain the diners. Perhaps, the singers were on a break which gave the two old friends time to catch up and reminisce. After they had done so for a while, Joshua spoke about some of his recent experiences,

"You Know Jim, what frustrates me often about living in the western world is the spiritual famine that so many suffer from. There is so much material stuff, so much to eat, so much more money in the pockets of many people but such a lack of spirituality in their lives.

People feel empty and they don't know why they feel empty. They think they are here once only and to get everything, do everything in a frantic race. Never searching, never realising who they really are: A spiritual being having an earthly experience."

Jim was a very good listener, it was one of his skills and one of the reasons why the two men got on so well.

Jim replied, "Yes, I agree with you. The trouble is in the west and here in a place like New York, what the fuck do you expect? The dollar is king! People here don't give a fuck about God......give me more money for fuck's sake!" Jim laughed loudly at his own words. He didn't give a dam about other people in restaurant overhearing their conversation, or his own raucous laugh. Why should he? He had survived a lonely winter living rough on the streets of New York. He had seen the indifference of most people first-hand in the city!

Joshua, laughed out loud too. Jim, always made him laugh, another reason Joshua enjoyed his irreverent company, he thought to himself.

Jim continued, "The consciousness of the nation reflects the values of the nation. Likewise, the choice of any President in power at any time reflects the attitudes of the country at that time. Don't you think so?"

Joshua replied, Yes, I think that is true. I myself miss the spiritual devotion of the people I met in Tibet, in India and even on the Reservation in Taos. They all still have a reverence for nature, for the Earth and for peace. I miss that, generally in England and the United States it seems that the people are hypnotised by trivia, by superficial matters and, they are fed one fear after another in the media which crushes their soul keeping them in fear and stopping their inner growth. I sometimes wonder if it is deliberate or perhaps the people who do it are themselves equally asleep?"

Jim replied, "A bit of both I think, Joshua. You either chase the dollar or you chase that spiritual peace within. They occupy different directions. But, the governments of the world want to make money for vested interests and the people are their workers or their slaves even, who they want to keep asleep to these truths in my opinion. They don't want them to wake up. It would spoil the party for the rich folk!"

Joshua listened and fell silent for a moment. He decided it was time to change the subject and lighten the mood. He wanted to have a laugh with Jim and hear all about his adventures in New York City. The city of dreams!

Joshua paid the bill and just as they left the restaurant the waiter started to sing 'A lullaby on Broadway' and they both laughed together. They headed for Central Park for a break from the constant traffic noise as they walked and talked along the wide walkways in the park with the tree canopies above they continued their talk.

Jim asked, "So, Joshua, after all these spiritual journeys have you found the answers that you have been seeking?"

Joshua, replied, "Yes, I have found some of the answers to some of my questions. Yes, I have! Right now, I am wondering about my destiny or rather what I should do with the rest of my life. I think that I have learnt a lot recently about my own spiritual nature and I feel that I want to share some of my own insights with others who are also looking for their own answers to life."

Jim was listening carefully to Joshua's answer and then replied, "I think you have something special about you Joshua. To me, you are a special person. Yes, I think you should try and help others, use your gifts, your skills, to show others and to help point them towards their own truth. Whether it is through what you write or say, your energy comes across either way. I think you could help a lot of people. All will be revealed in time. Ask and pray when you meditate for the answers that you are seeking. You will get there I am sure. I think you are on the right path."

Joshua, replied, "Thank you Jim for your advice here. I think I needed some reassurance right now because I do doubt myself a lot of the time which can be frustrating. I have struggled with a lack of self-belief in the past but I am definitely growing in confidence I feel now."

"You will get there just wait and see, I am sure of that!" Jim replied.

***

Joshua decided to spend a few more days in New York with Jim often walking around with the skyscrapers towering high above them in a city populated by so many people seeking their fortune rather than what makes their own soul sing.

On one such day, Jim took Joshua to meet a friend of his called 'Lazlo', who Jim thought was an unusual person for some reason. He had met Lazlo during his time that he spent living on the streets and during his first winter in the city. Lazlo was from the city of Marrakesh in Morocco and had worked in the markets or 'Souks' as they are known there, as a snake charmer and had his own market stall. He had run a business too, taking tourist to the Atlas Mountains near Marrakesh.

Lazlo, was seventy-five years old and with a distinctive Arabic appearance, he had been born in

Tunisia during the second world war. His parents had been resistance fighters there against the Nazi invaders. Lazlo, was too young then to remember such things but his parents had told him many stories about some of the events from that period in their own lives, stories of heroism and danger fighting for the sake of the future of their own country.

Lazlo, had the air of someone however, who had not always lived a good and honest life. Indeed, he had not and a certain event in his own life ended up showing him the error of his ways and causing him to lose all his money in New York. This had involved a shady deal with the Mafia in the city which led to him having to hide through disappearing and living anonymously on the streets of the city and how Jim had come to meet up with Lazlo when he first arrived in the city. During that cold winter, they had both become friends and Lazlo told Jim many tales about his own life.

Lazlo, by this time ran his own small coffee shop on the Lower East Side of the City.

"This is Lazlo, Joshua," said Jim.

Joshua, looked Lazlo directly in the eyes having heard the stories about him from his friend Jim. Lazlo, was short, obese and bald, he had a greying beard and long wispy hair which looked like it was never combed.

"Nice to meet you Joshua. I have heard a lot about you. Jim has told me about some of the places that you have been recently. I hear that you are a bit of a mystic. Is that right Joshua?" Lazlo asked.

"I am a seeker of the truth, yes," replied Joshua.

Lazlo, gave them both a coffee and some cake to eat on the house. He was the owner of the business after all and so he took off his apron and sat down to join them at their table.

Lazlo continued to speak to them, "Jim is very tough. He survived a New York winter on the streets, as did I a few years ago. Did he tell you about that, Joshua? I guess he did."

He did tell me about it a bit," said Joshua, a bit sheepishly.

Lazlo said to them both, "It was tough. Darn tough. Not many have the metal, the resilience to not go under. You feel often like no more than dirt under a person's shoe. You are invisible to nearly all of society. It teaches you how hard life can be. New York is one of the hardest, coldest meanest places on Earth! But is also one of the most beautiful if you have plenty of money. I now have plenty of money once more. But I had to pull myself up by my own boot-straps and not for the first time I might add!

My story lies in how I got the money to buy this café, having previously lost everything. Would you like to hear my story, Joshua? Or, has Jim already told you?"

"No, Jim has not told me that story," replied Joshua.

Lazlo continued, "Well, what happened was, I saw a man shoot another man dead one night in a street in China Town. I guessed it was over a drugs deal. I am not sure of the reason. Most people there would have disappeared into the night and remained silent, like the murderer did. I chose not to. It felt right to me – I contacted the police, they attended, did their investigation and caught the offender from the information I gave them about him. I attended court, he was found guilty and put away for life. I in turn thereafter started to receive death threats from the Mafia. I changed my appearance and thought the safest thing to do, would be to hide under their noses, by living on the streets here for a year or so. That's what I did. That is how I met Jim.

I lost everything, I had in that time, one day when I was asleep I was woken up by a passer-by. He didn't speak. He just smiled at me. His eyes were the strangest colour ever. They were violet in colour. He looked like an angel in normal clothes. He gave me an envelope. After he left. Well, just disappeared really, right in front of my eyes. I opened the envelope. I opened it only to find a million dollars in one thousand dollar bills or what you might call notes. They were worth even more because they are now so rare but still legal tender.

I never found out who the guy was but he looked like some kind of Angel and I swear to you, he disappeared right in front of my eyes!

In case you ask I am tee-total! I have been all my life. I am a Muslim and a proud one, Joshua! I used the money to get off the street and buy this small café. It was one year to the day when I received the money after the shooting I witnessed, it was as if it happened perhaps, because I was brave enough to be a witness to the murder. Otherwise I have no other explanation! I have not been an angel in my own life Joshua, though I never did anything really bad, I never really hurt another!"

Joshua, was silent for a while, then replied, "That is some story. Sometimes incredible things happen to us for no apparent reason. I can only guess that as well as that good deed that you did that you also did something special in another life! Or, perhaps it was because of the good your parents did during the Second World War perhaps, Lazlo?"

"Yes, maybe. Can I get you guys another coffee?" replied Lazlo.

***

Lazlo, returned with a coffee for each of them and continued with his story, "I realise how special this gift was for me for whatever reason. I decided in having the money to buy this business I should help other poor people, however I could. Often, in the course of a day several people who know about me and who are destitute will come into the coffee shop and I will give them a free drink and a free meal. This is one of my ways for paying back for what I received. Some of the down-trodden individuals who come here for my help have been coming here for a few years now."

Joshua, replied, "That is very kind of you and I am sure those people greatly appreciate your help Lazlo."

Lazlo replied, "Well thank you Joshua, but I feel it is the least I can do in return following my good fortune."

Jim said to them both, "I was one of those people Lazlo helped, when he got this coffee shop I was still living on the street. I was one of those grateful people he helped. Wasn't I Lazlo?"

"You were indeed Jim and you were one of the people who told others about this place to the poor and customers alike," replied Lazlo.

Jim and Joshua thanked Lazlo for sharing his amazing story and both bid him farewell and left the coffee shop.

As they walked along the side-walk and along the busy streets of the city Jim turned to Joshua and said, "I would like to be able to perform miracles. You know make stuff appear out of thin air like that weird guy who turned up out of nowhere and gave him a million dollars in thousand dollar bills and then just vanished. Like some of the things you told me about witnessing yourself in India. Wouldn't that be cool?"

Joshua was, as often was the case, quiet and contemplated for a while before answering, then said,

"If you could perform such acts it would not be thought of as cool by the person doing such things. I don't think a person who did such things would do it out of ego but to help others in some way. I think that would have to be a part of it. That the person had evolved that much and realised that such an altruistic act would have to have a higher purpose than for mere entertainment or to show off. I would like to be able to do such things myself. But I feel that right now my ego would still be a big factor in wishing to be able to do such a thing!"

"Okay, but if you did it to only help others, wouldn't that mean it was okay?" asked Jim.

"Yes, perhaps, but it would be about the underlying reason or purpose of such," replied Joshua.

"How do you know when you have evolved to that level and purpose?" asked Jim.

Joshua replied, "I think when the teacher has showed up to show you the way. I think that would be a key sign."

"Has your teacher showed up yet to show you how to perform miracles Joshua?" asked Jim.

"I don't think so yet!" replied Joshua.

As he gave the answer to the question, Papa Luca, Joshua's mysterious friend, who just seemed to appear now and again and disappear, popped up in Joshua's mind. Joshua thought to himself for a moment. Maybe

Papa Luca was such a person? He let the though pass and kept it to himself.

***

The two old friends enjoyed walking the busy sidewalks in silence observing the crowds of people as they hurried through their day from place to place and as the constant flow of traffic passed through the busy concrete canyons which channelled the wind like the Tibetan Mountain valley where Joshua had so recently been and to them both, New York City was equally as breathtaking, mysterious and exciting in so many ways, including the tales of strange spiritual events like the one they had just been told by Lazlo.

***

On Joshua's last day in New York, Jim accompanied him on the overland train back to the JFK International Airport for his flight back to England. On his return flight, he reflected on his trip to the United states of America, he thought about his time at both places he had visited. Taos and the Reservation with White Eagle Feather and his time spent with Jim in the city and his meeting with Lazlo. Joshua, felt a deep gratitude for all the things he had learnt on his trip and for the mystical experiences he had there and the stories he was told.

Once back home, life soon settled back into its normal routine for Joshua. He caught up with his friends and enjoyed the tranquillity that the ocean brought to him. Although Joshua spent most days in his home town, he enjoyed the fact that it always looked different, whether through the vista of the sea or the sky. He enjoyed the sense of space this gave to him, but he mostly enjoyed being part of a community and the sense of belonging this gave to him.

One day having been back home for several weeks, Joshua was joined again by his old friend Papa Luca in the usual haunt such meetings took place, being the Galley café.

Papa Luca took a seat next to Joshua, while Joshua was deep in thought,

"Can I join you Joshua, a penny for your thoughts. How are you my friend?" Papa Luca enquired.

"Oh, Papa Luca, how nice to see you! I have not seen you for a long time. How are you?" replied Joshua.

Papa Luca replied, "I am well Joshua. I hear you have had more adventures. This time in America, if I am not mistaken?"

"Yes, that is right. I returned just a few weeks ago," replied Joshua.

"And what new spiritual insights did you take from this most recent adventure of yours then Joshua?" enquired Papa Luca.

Joshua paused to think for a quite a long time before answering his old friends question. He knew that this was rather like an exam question and that a careful reply would be expected.

"I learnt to saviour the moment more and to be grateful for that as much as possible," replied Joshua.

Then continued, "I realised more how none of us are here in this life for long even if we live to be one hundred years old because even that length of time passes quickly and is a speck of time in relation to the existence of this planet of ours. I realised how I yearn for deeper and deeper spiritual insights, probably at a much greater speed than my mind is ready for. I would for instance like to be able to perform miracles, like Jesus did, but I realise that comes more from my ego more than to help others! I realise that because that is the case, I am not likely to be able to do such things unless I fully integrate that knowing into my being.

I am realising just the fact we are alive is a miracle. The fact if we are healthy, that is a miracle, and that some of us can procreate and the female of the species gives birth to another human being; that is one of the greatest miracles. I am learning to be more grateful for what I already have and have had, for most of my life to date. I am learning to be more appreciative for all those things!"

"That is good, Joshua. Sometimes it takes a long time to have these types of insights. But you are right of course. You are learning to be happy with what you already have in so many ways and to accept what will be, will be. That takes wisdom," replied Papa Luca.

Papa Luca finished his coffee, bid Joshua farewell and left the café and just seemed to disappear somehow, soon after leaving the Galley Café. Joshua, smiled to himself and gave thanks to the universe for these simple but important new insights that had come to him in his own life.

***

The next day, the sun was shining and there was little wind blowing. Joshua, knew that the tide was high at the time. It was by then the month of May and the weather was warm and the evenings had become longer. Much had happened in Joshua's life in the previous year.

Joshua, opened his bedroom cupboard drawer once more and looked at the old map with the mysterious cross on it and marked near the location of the estuary entrance a few miles down the coast from his home town. He remembered his trip, made on a whim, an impulse, to visit 'x' marks the spot. He remembered the dolphin which appeared when Harry the boat skipper and he made the journey there not really expecting to find anything. How could he? It was not as if he planned to scuba-dive for treasure, he thought to himself! He had no such intention. Maybe, all that he was meant to do was to see and appreciate the dolphin that greeted him there on that day. Anyway, Joshua, liked boats a lot and he was always eager to get out on the sea, even if it only was for a short time and a short journey because he liked it so much, if he didn't get sea-sickness of course!

He decided to walk down to the harbour to see if Harry was free to take him back there. On arrival, by good fortune Harry was alone on his boat moored by the harbour wall, "Hello, Harry. How are you?" enquired Joshua.

"Oh, hello, Joshua. Long-time no see!" replied Harry, smiling with his usual cheerful demeanour.

Harry continued, "Where have you been? What have you been up to then Joshua? It feels like a year since I saw you last. I remember, it was that wild goose chase out to the estuary with you and that old map. All we found was a dolphin! Although I'll admit, something I only see on occasion. A good omen they say, seeing one of those you know!"

Joshua replied, "I think you might be right. I have been on quite a few adventures since that day and on reflection almost as if the dolphin was the start of them all! I can tell you all about it, if you let me join you on your boat for a while today?"

"Okay, then. I am going to be out for a few hours checking my lobster pots. I might even end up going down to that estuary again too, as I have a pot down near to it. Hop on board then!" replied Harry with a big grin on his face.

Joshua climbed aboard the small fishing boat and soon together they were sailing out of the small harbour into the open sea. Fortunately for Joshua his sea-sickness stayed away on this occasion.

"So, what have you been up to then?" enquired Harry curiously, speaking with his usual West Country accent.

"Harry, I have been all over the world. I've spent time in India with a spiritual teacher. Also, I have spent time in Tibet, in two different monasteries, with some very wise monks. I spent time in New Mexico in America visiting a Medicine Man and his son on a Reservation. Finally, I spent a bit of time on my return with my old friend Jim in New York. He lived here once, a few years ago."

"So, in other words, you have been pretty busy then, my old friend," replied Harry.

"Yes, I guess so. I have learnt a lot too!" replied Joshua.

"What sort of stuff did you learn then?" Harry enquired.

"Well, how long have you got?" replied Joshua.

"Well, I am not sure if I can listen to all that mumbo-jumbo stuff you seem to be interested in. I don't care about it much really! As long as I can keep on catching fish each day to pay my bills and buy a few beers now and again I am happy! I like the simple life, Joshua. That's it really!" replied Harry.

"There is nothing wrong with that Harry. There is a lot to be said for having a simple life. Living in the moment and with few worries. I suppose in a way, that was one of the things I learnt and has stuck in my mind the most about my recent travels," said Joshua.

"Yes, I do like to keep my life simple!" replied Harry smiling with his eyes twinkling.

The small fishing boat sailed on from lobster pot to lobster pot. The two men stayed silent for most of the journey just being peaceful and in the moment. Joshua, though could not help at times thinking about many of the things that he had seen and done in the months that had just passed. As he gazed from the boat out to sea towards the estuary not far in front and close to where he had visited with Harry nearly twelve months previous he suddenly noticed the fins of a pod of dolphins a short distance from the boat. Harry was busy pulling up a lobster pot. Suddenly, on the opposite side of the boat to which Harry was facing Joshua saw six dolphins leap simultaneously several feet up out of the sea. The dolphins seemed to Joshua not only to be smiling but as if they were also dancing somehow in mid-air as they leapt out of the water. Joshua, could not believe what he had just seen. He looked over at Harry and saw he was probably too busy pulling up his lobster pots to notice them.

"Harry, Harry, did you just see that?

Dolphins loads of them. Did you see them?" shouted Joshua with excitement in his voice!

"No, I didn't see anything!" Harry replied.

THE END

If you enjoyed this book, which I hope you did of course and would like it to reach the hearts and minds of others to hopefully inspire them too, then please leave a brief review about the book on the site you purchased it from to help draw others to this books story and message too for their inspiration. Thank you. Love and light to you all! Simon Herfet.

Printed in Great Britain
by Amazon

48235126R00128